D1645366

9030 00007 6839 9

The Girl
Who Talked
to Trees

First published in the UK in 2021 by Zephyr
an imprint of Head of Zeus Ltd

Text copyright © Natasha Farrant 2021
Artwork copyright © Lydia Corry 2021

The moral right of Natasha Farrant to be identified as the author and
Lydia Corry to be indentified as the artist of this work has been asserted in
accordance with the Copyright, Designs and Patents Act of 1988.

All rights reserved.

No part of this publication may be reproduced, stored in a retrieval system,
or transmitted in any form or by any means, electronic, mechanical,
photocopying, recording, or otherwise, without the prior permission of both
the copyright owner and the above publisher of this book.

This is a work of fiction. All characters, organisations, and events portrayed
in this novel are either products of the author's imagination or are used
fictitiously.

9 7 5 3 1 2 4 6 8

A catalogue record for this book is available from the British Library.

ISBN (HB): 9781800242234
ISBN (E): 9781800242258

Designed by Jessie Price

Printed and bound in Slovenia by DZS Grafik.

Head of Zeus Ltd
First Floor East
5–8 Hardwick Street
London EC1R 4RG
www.headofzeus.com

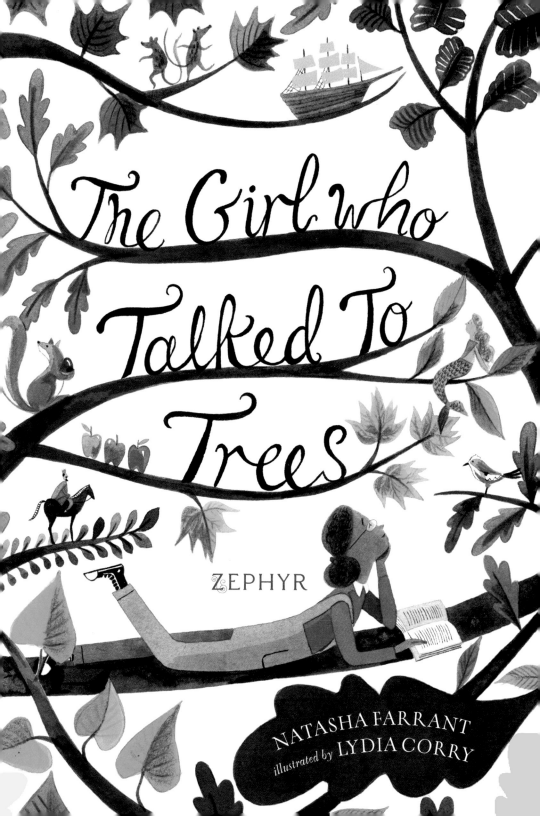

The Girl who Talked To Trees

ZEPHYR

NATASHA FARRANT

illustrated by LYDIA CORRY

LONDON BOROUGH OF WANDSWORTH	
9030 00007 6839 9	
Askews & Holts	
JF	
	WW21011838

For Sammy and Victor.
- NF

For my mother, Sally,
with all my love.
- LC

CONTENTS

TULIP TREE

ELM TREE

BOX WOOD

PLANE TREE

OAK TREE

GREAT HOUSE

APPLE ORCHARD

BIRCH WOOD

ALDER TREES

LINDEN TREE

The Girl Who Talked to Trees

I n a secret valley not so very far away from here, there sits a famous old house. It is a grand sort of place, with tall pillars and lots of chimneys and a clock tower, but that is not what it is famous for.

It is famous for its trees.

The house stands in parkland at the top of a hill. It looks on to a big lawn dotted with beech, an elm and - of course - the splendid tulip tree. The lawn slopes to a river lined with hornbeam, willow and alder. There is a walled orchard in the park too, with a dozen different sorts of apples. Over the bridge, opposite the house, is a wood full of oak, lime, hazel and box. It is a small wood these days, but once upon a time it was a great forest – the hunting ground of a prince!

Sometimes, if you listen carefully, it's almost as though you can hear voices among the trees.

One day – it is said – they will grant a wish... to the right person.

Which is where our story begins, with a girl called Olive.

Olive was eleven years old, not very tall, with hair in pigtails and little wire glasses which often slipped down her nose. She was clever and kind and extremely shy, and her best friend was a four-hundred-year-old oak tree.

'A tree?' you say. 'How strange.'

But think about it.

When you are so shy you dare not even look at anyone in case they want to talk to you – or worse, want you to talk to them – a tree is a very sensible choice for a friend.

Broad and comfortable, Olive's oak stood alone in a meadow on the hillside opposite the house. She spent most of her spare time in its company, reading or drawing or simply lying on a branch, watching things. Olive, who rarely spoke to anyone, told the oak tree everything. When she was sad, it soothed her with its rocking. When she was happy, its leaves rustled with a sound like laughter.

Sometimes she hugged it.

Her family didn't understand.

'Here comes Olive, back from talking to her tree!' her bossy sister Rosa would say, as Olive trudged up the lawn with twigs sticking out of her hair. 'I do worry our Olive is going to turn into a tree,' her mother, Lady Josephine, told visitors while Sir Sydney, her father, shook his head. Even Nana was concerned. 'I like trees too, dear,' she told Olive, 'but you should have human friends.'

The servants secretly called her the Girl Who Talked to Trees.

But everyone loved her, so on the whole they didn't interfere – until breakfast one sunny spring morning, when her father announced that he had a New Plan.

His family looked warily at each other. Sir Sydney often had New Plans, and they always meant Chaos and Disruption.

'I have decided,' Sir Sydney declared, 'to build a new house.'

'But we already have a house, dear,' reasoned Lady Jo.

'Not to live in,' said Sir Sydney. 'A summerhouse! For parties and picnics.'

'How much would it cost?' Lady Jo was much more sensible than her husband.

Sir Sydney waved his hand, as if to say, 'What is money compared to parties and picnics?'

'I will build it in the meadow,' he said.

The meadow! thought Olive.

'Think about it!' cried Sir Sydney. 'Summer evenings, the moon, the stars... looking back over the valley, the park all lit up... It would be impressive.'

Sir Sydney was a man who liked to impress.

Olive screwed up the courage to speak.

'Where exactly in the meadow?' she asked.

Her father shifted on his chair, and Olive knew, she just knew.

'Where my oak tree is,' she said.

Sir Sydney nodded. 'I'm sorry about that. But there are lots of other trees.'

'Not like mine,' said Olive. 'The oak tree is my friend.'

Everybody stared, even the servants. It was rare enough to hear Olive talk, let alone stand up to her father. And possibly because he was so surprised, Sir Sydney said, 'Very well. I have to go out now, but I will be back at teatime. If by then you can think of something more impressive than my summerhouse, I will not cut down the oak.'

'Do you promise?' asked Olive.

'I promise.' Sir Sydney looked at his watch. 'You have just over seven hours.'

'I'll do it!' Olive vowed. 'I will think of something!'

She ran out of the breakfast room, down the big lawn, over the bridge and through the woods to the meadow, where all her determination left her and she crumpled at the foot of her oak tree.

She had no idea what to do next.

The wind breathed through the oak tree's branches. Olive curled up among its roots.

'I wish you would help me,' she said.

The oak leaves sighed.

The trees in the woods sighed.

Olive began to feel drowsy. She closed her eyes and yawned. She mustn't sleep... she mustn't... she had to think.

She slept.

The clock in the tower struck the hour.

When Olive woke, the meadow, the oak, and the view of the valley were gone.

Oak forests support more life forms than any other forest – over 2300 birds, mammals, insects, moss and fungi depend on them.

There are about 500 species of oak tree.

They grow 20–40 metres tall.

They usually live to between 100 and 300 years, but can live to well over 1000.

Every autumn jays bury thousands of acorns to use as food in the winter – some of which grow into new trees!

COMMON OAK

Quercus Robur

Oak

live was lying on the floor of a forest and a voice was shouting in her ear. She scrambled to her knees and looked around, but there was nobody there.

What was this place? She had never seen a forest like it, so close and full, so alive. Vast trees soared above her, blocking out the sun, draped in vines and moss, with giant fungi growing from their trunks and a tangle of smaller trees spread beneath them. And the noise! Creaking branches and rustling leaves, the caw of rooks and the rat-a-tat of woodpeckers, the trill and chatter of songbirds. In every forest Olive had ever visited there were always some signs of human activity – a coppiced tree, the glimpse of a

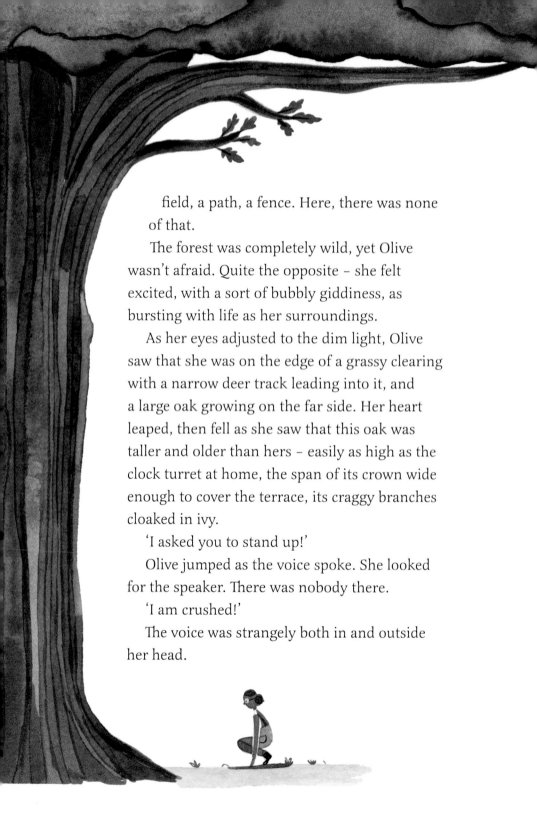

field, a path, a fence. Here, there was none
of that.

The forest was completely wild, yet Olive
wasn't afraid. Quite the opposite – she felt
excited, with a sort of bubbly giddiness, as
bursting with life as her surroundings.

As her eyes adjusted to the dim light, Olive
saw that she was on the edge of a grassy clearing
with a narrow deer track leading into it, and
a large oak growing on the far side. Her heart
leaped, then fell as she saw that this oak was
taller and older than hers – easily as high as the
clock turret at home, the span of its crown wide
enough to cover the terrace, its craggy branches
cloaked in ivy.

'I asked you to stand up!'

Olive jumped as the voice spoke. She looked
for the speaker. There was nobody there.

'I am crushed!'

The voice was strangely both in and outside
her head.

This is mad, thought Olive.

Pushing herself into a crouch, she peered at the ground where she had been kneeling.

Dead leaves, a few mushrooms, an enormous orange slug...

'Is that you?' she asked.

There was a shocked silence, followed by an icy, 'No.'

'Can't you wave or something?'

Another chilly silence.

'Not without help,' the voice said.

As if on cue, a gust of wind blew through the clearing. The trees swayed. The dead leaves which covered the forest floor lifted and fell.

'You must be able to
see me now,' said the voice.
'I am waving at you!'
Olive peered again.

'I see a... twig?'

'A twig?'

'More of a seedling,' said Olive. 'Like a very tiny
tree...'

An idea crept into her head, so startling and huge
she screwed her eyes tight shut to make it go away. It
couldn't be. It was impossible! Cautiously, she opened
her eyes again. The seedling was still there, no higher
than her knee, with a slim stem as green as grass,
and at the end of that stem two very
familiar-looking leaves...

Olive sat back down with
a thump.

'I think you're my oak,'
she said in a daze.

'Your oak?' The tiny
tree swelled in the breeze,

making it look briefly bigger. 'I belong to nobody.'

How? Olive hugged her knees, thinking. What exactly had happened before she woke up here? She had argued with her father... run to the oak, crumpled at its feet...

Asked for its help...

Was it possible?

'You shrank,' she said.

'SHRANK?'

Olive turned back to the little tree.

'I think,' she said, 'I may have travelled back in time.'

'That makes a lot more sense,' said the little tree, and Olive thought it sounded relieved. 'So where you came from...'

'Where I came from, you are huge,' she assured it.

'How huge?' demanded the seedling. 'Am I the biggest tree in the forest?'

Olive thought of her tree's lonely meadow and decided not to mention that.

'Am I magnificent?' the little tree asked.

Before Olive could answer, a clamour of rooks took off from the high branches of the ancient oak, and a new sound sliced through the forest.

It was the piercing call of a hunting horn.

A doe bounded into the clearing and paused, pricked her ears to listen then vanished back into the trees. Olive jumped to her feet. Suddenly, she was afraid, with a choking dread which rose from the ground, rose and spread through her limbs and all over her body.

In the distance, she heard the excited howl of hounds.

'The hunt approaches.' A new voice, deeper than the seedling's, wove in and out of Olive's head. 'You are not safe.'

'It is the Old One speaking,' whispered the seedling. 'On the edge of the clearing.'

The ancient oak... Olive ran to it.

'What must I do?'

'Climb,' said the new voice.

Olive hesitated. The oak was so ancient, so grand – the thought of climbing it felt disrespectful.

The hunting horn sounded again, followed by the frenzied barking of hounds. Olive seized a rope of ivy with both hands and pulled herself up.

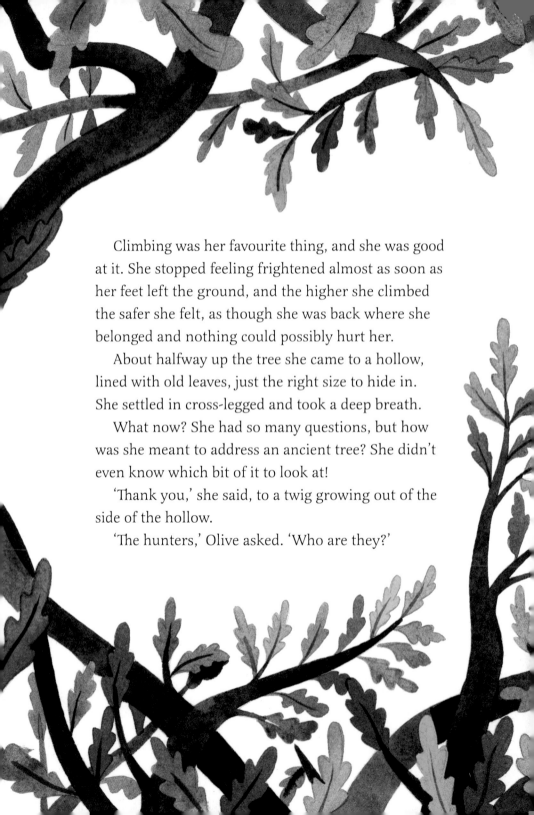

Climbing was her favourite thing, and she was good at it. She stopped feeling frightened almost as soon as her feet left the ground, and the higher she climbed the safer she felt, as though she was back where she belonged and nothing could possibly hurt her.

About halfway up the tree she came to a hollow, lined with old leaves, just the right size to hide in. She settled in cross-legged and took a deep breath.

What now? She had so many questions, but how was she meant to address an ancient tree? She didn't even know which bit of it to look at!

'Thank you,' she said, to a twig growing out of the side of the hollow.

'The hunters,' Olive asked. 'Who are they?'

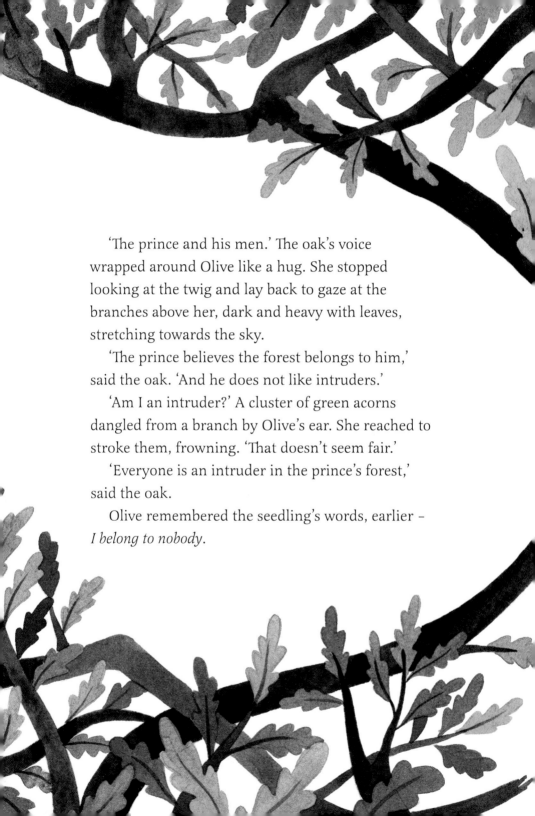

'The prince and his men.' The oak's voice wrapped around Olive like a hug. She stopped looking at the twig and lay back to gaze at the branches above her, dark and heavy with leaves, stretching towards the sky.

'The prince believes the forest belongs to him,' said the oak. 'And he does not like intruders.'

'Am I an intruder?' A cluster of green acorns dangled from a branch by Olive's ear. She reached to stroke them, frowning. 'That doesn't seem fair.'

'Everyone is an intruder in the prince's forest,' said the oak.

Olive remembered the seedling's words, earlier – *I belong to nobody.*

'Is it really the prince's forest?' she asked.

'He likes to think so,' said the oak. 'As if a forest can be owned! But, hush… here is the hunters' prey.'

Olive leaned forward to peep through the ivy.

A boy stood in the middle of the clearing, barefoot, dressed in a torn tunic and breeches. Olive couldn't see his face at first because he was bent double with his hands on his knees, but then he straightened and she saw that he was about her age.

She frowned again.

'I don't understand,' she said. 'Who is he?'

'Just a boy,' sighed the oak.

'But what is he doing here?'

'The prince does not like intruders,' the oak repeated.

The hounds were drawing closer. Olive heard human voices now among their howls, and the pounding of horses' hooves. Her spine prickled. The boy stood frozen in the middle of the clearing. He had heard them too.

'What will the hunters do if they catch him?'

The tree did not answer. Olive gripped the edge of the hollow.

'Up here!' she shouted. 'Use the ivy to climb!'

But the boy did not look up. Olive reached for the acorns above her head and pulled three off.

'Sorry,' she said to the tree, and took aim.

The first two acorns missed. The third hit the boy square on top of his head. He started and looked up.

'CLIMB!' Olive yelled.

And the boy obeyed.

Up he came, while Olive kept an anxious watch for the hunters.

'In here!' she whispered as he reached her hiding place.

Wordlessly, the boy slid in beside her. She reached to squeeze his shoulder.

Her hand went straight through him.

'He does not hear you,' the oak murmured as Olive stared. 'No human can. Only us, and...'

Closer and closer, the hounds bayed.

Still disbelieving, she passed her hand back and forth in front of the boy's face. He didn't even blink.

'But he heard me,' she said. 'I know he did.'

'He felt the acorn that you threw,' said the oak. 'It is another way of hearing. But quiet now... they are here.'

And the hunt burst into the clearing.

A dozen hounds spilled out of the forest, followed by two riders, both men, the first, the prince himself, on a black gelding, the second on a grey mare. Unlike the hunted boy, they were finely dressed, and in excellent spirits.

'Where did he go?' The prince wheeled his horse about the clearing as the dogs sniffed the grass. In the hollow next to Olive, the boy curled into a ball, making himself as small as possible.

A wolfhound howled and bounded to the oak, scrabbling at the trunk. His companions surged around him.

The boy gave a tiny whine of fear.

Olive sat very still.

The prince leaped from his horse and strode towards the oak.

'Footprints!' the prince cried, pointing at the grass. 'And see how the ivy here has come away from the trunk? Someone has been climbing...'

He threw back his head.

'Come down, lad!' he shouted. 'It will be better for you if you do!'

The boy curled himself tighter.

Olive balled her fists.

The other horseman dismounted. The two men talked, too quietly for Olive to hear. The prince appeared to be giving orders. The second seemed to protest, but after a short discussion he nodded, then remounted and cantered out of the clearing on the same path they had entered by.

'Where is he going?' Olive asked.

The creak of the oak's branches sounded like weeping.

They waited. The oak. The prince at the foot of the oak with the hounds and the black gelding. Olive and the boy in their hiding place.

Quiet at first but getting louder and louder, Olive heard new voices muttering as the forest waited with them.

Something bad was coming, she could feel it.

Something very bad.

When at last they returned, the grey mare and her rider were not alone. Another man walked behind them, carrying an axe...

The first blow fell.

The oak shuddered.

Olive cried out, but no one heard her.

Another blow, and as the ancient oak tree groaned the voices of the forest grew louder.

'Promise,' they whispered in creaks and rustles. 'Promise on your life.'

'Promise what?' whispered Olive.

'That when the time comes, you will protect us. They will laugh at you. They will call you a child and say you do not understand but you must speak, louder and louder until they listen.'

Olive swallowed. 'I'm not very good at talking to humans.'

'You will
find a way to be
heard.'

The woodcutter raised his
axe for the third blow.

'Promise,' sang
the trees.

'I promise,' she said and was surprised at
how firm she sounded.

'Promise what?'

'When the time comes, I will protect you. I will
speak, louder and louder until people listen.
I promise on my life.'

The blow struck, but Olive didn't hear it. The
barking of the dogs melted away, the cawing of the
rooks, the creaks and rustles of the trees. An eerie
silence fell over the forest, an absolute stillness.

The storm began gently, with the shifting of leaves
on the forest floor.

The shift became a swell, the swell rippled, and
suddenly sound was back. The dogs howled, the
horses neighed. Overhead, rooks screamed the alarm
as the forest floor, like an ocean wave, began to rise
and fall.

Olive and the boy clung to the sides of their hollow, but not a leaf of the great oak moved, not a branch, not a twig. Olive glanced at the other trees and saw that they too were still.

What sort of a storm affected only the forest floor?

Far below, the ground heaved, then erupted as a root broke through, raining earth as it snaked across the clearing towards the dogs. It coiled around a terrified wolfhound and hurled it across the clearing.

The wolfhound whimpered, then leaped to its feet and fled, followed by the rest of the pack. The horses bolted. The forest let them go, but it was not so gentle

with the men. Another root erupted, and another. Again and again, the men tried to run. Again and again, they were thrown down, until at last the forest seemed to have had enough. With a final heave, it threw the woodcutter out of the clearing. Two roots curled around the two riders and raised them high. For an awful moment, Olive thought it was going to crush them. But then they too were flung away. The storm ended as suddenly as it had started. The ground closed, the forest floor was still. A whirlwind of leaves collapsed with a *swoooosh.*

Olive drew a breath.

'What just happened?' she whispered.

The oak was silent.

A few minutes later, when he was sure the hunters would not return, the shaking boy climbed down from the tree. Olive watched him go. She did not think that he would look back, but when he reached the path he turned to gaze straight up at where she was sitting and placed his hand on his heart.

Olive raised her own hand in response.

And then he was gone.

Olive stayed a while longer.

'Can I ask a question?' she said. 'It's a little bit awkward, but I would like to know.'

The oak tree's branches swayed.

'In my time, where I came from... you're not there. What happened to you?'

The branches danced, but when it spoke the oak tree's voice was grave.

'Everything has a time to die, even great trees,' it said. 'Yet, in a way, am I not there? Look across the clearing. What do you see?'

Olive looked. 'I see the grass and trees. I see the path and dead leaves, and if I narrow my eyes I see my tiny oak... no, not my tiny oak, that's wrong, I mean the tiny oak and... oh! Oh, I see! I do see!'

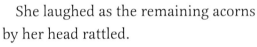

She laughed as the remaining acorns by her head rattled.

'The tiny oak grew from one of your acorns. Oh, I'm so glad!'

'And now you must go,' the oak said gently. 'You must find the next tree.'

'What next tree?' said Olive. 'What do you mean?'

'Seven hours for seven trees, and seven stories to tell...' The oak's voice was slipping away. 'They will help you keep your promise.'

'But how?' pressed Olive. 'Where are they? How will I know them?'

Far away across the valley, a clock chimed. The oak tree did not answer. Olive guessed that it would not speak again.

A yellow flower floated towards her, caught on a breeze. Olive reached for it but it whirled away.

'Follow me!' it seemed to say.

Olive climbed down and went after it into the forest.

Bees love linden flowers and make honey from them, but their pollen contains a sugar which makes the bees drowsy if they have too much.

There are about
30 species of linden.

They grow 20-40 metres
(but can be taller).

Like the oak, they
usually live 100-300 years,
but can live over 1000.

Look out for bees napping under the trees!

LINDEN

Talia

Linden

The linden tree was like a castle, the sort with fortifications for pouring hot oil out of and narrow slits for shooting arrows. There is a word for castles like that: impregnable. It means unconquerable. Impossible to capture.

Olive had never seen a tree so solid or so huge. She walked around it and tried to count her steps, but gave up when she reached fifty, tipped her head back and looked up. She blinked. Shafts of sunlight shone through gaps in the linden's crown, dazzlingly bright, a world away from the shadows of the forest floor.

What must it be like up there?

'You can see for ever.' The tree's voice was unexpectedly soft, wrapping around Olive like feathers, making her feel strangely weightless. 'Climb and I will show you.'

Olive didn't think twice and began to climb. There was no ivy rope here, but the linden's knotty trunk offered plenty of hand and footholds to help her. She reached the first branches. They were broad and massive, stretching so far she couldn't see where they ended. It would take days to explore a tree like this. Weeks!

Up Olive went and the higher she went, the brighter the light became and the higher she wanted to go. The branches grew slimmer and began to dip beneath her weight, but Olive didn't stop until one almost gave way completely and she slipped back down, landing with a series of bumps a few branches below.

It took her a few seconds to wriggle to a
safe position and catch her breath. Then she gazed
again at the sunlight shining through the leaves.

How could she reach it?

The linden swayed, the breeze tickling her neck.

'There is a way,' it sang. 'But it is dangerous. Shall
I tell you?'

Olive glanced at the ground and rubbed her arm,
where already a bruise was forming.

'There is a greater danger than falling,' the linden
murmured. 'Shall I tell you anyway?'

Olive looked once more at the ground. She could
climb down now, and be safe... But then she looked
again at the glimpses of sky above.

'Tell me,' she said.

And the linden began its story.

ᵛONCE THERE WAS A BOY CALLED LUCA.

He lived with his parents in a big city, where there was always something fun and exciting to do, and he loved it there. But one winter, when he was eleven years old, a new sickness came to the city. His mother caught it and fell gravely ill, and the doctor recommended that the family move to the country, where fresh air and quiet would make her better.

And so they came here.

Luca's parents loved the country. His mother sat in the garden and grew stronger every day. His father read a lot. Only Luca hated it. Homesick for the city, with no brothers or sisters, no friends to play with, he was bored and lonely. In time he grew grumpy and sulky.

'Why don't you go out and explore?' his parents urged, as Luca skulked about the house, dragging his feet and slamming doors. 'There's a whole forest to discover!'

But Luca was not interested in exploring. Months passed and he barely set foot in the garden. Spring arrived, and his father lost patience.

'If you can't enjoy being here,' he said, 'we will have to send you away to school.'

'It's lovely here, darling,' his mother said gently. 'Come out with me into the garden and I'll show you.'

Luca didn't want to go away to school, and he
didn't want to look at the garden. So out he went
into the forest, but he hated it too. Hated the birds
and their giddy springtime singing, the stupid fluffy
lambs in the fields and the big-eyed calves. Hated
the cheerful flowers which reminded him of how
miserable he was, far away from his friends and the
life he loved.

He walked slowly at first, kicking stones along the path. Then, because kicking wasn't enough to relieve his sad heart, he ran.

Luca ran, and he ran, and he ran, faster and further than he had ever run in his life. He didn't stop until he came to the heart of the forest, where he threw himself at the foot of a giant tree.

Luca sniffed. A tear rolled down his cheek.

'I wish someone would help me,' he whispered.

He closed his eyes.

Far away, a clock chimed...

The forest had been dark and gloomy when Luca fell asleep. His first thought on waking was how bright it was. And how had he missed so much detail before? The tiny flowers on a mossy path, the vivid green bug on a blade of grass.

His second thought was how loud the forest was. Not just the yelling birds, but the shift and twitch of leaves, the hum of ladybirds' wings… And the smells! Sweet sap and tender leaves, the delicate scent of linden flowers. Further away, carried on the breeze, something dangerous…

Everything was so…

BIG.

Luca knew before he looked that he was different too. Hardly daring, he gazed down at himself...

Instead of hands, he saw sharp-clawed, long-fingered paws. He curled in his chin and saw a bib of white fur. Twisted his neck and saw, curling over soft red fur, the plume of a feathery tail...

'Climb.'

The voice was unlike anything Luca had ever heard before, in and outside his head, strong but light as air. Luca knew without question that it was coming from the tree.

He tried to speak but his mouth couldn't form words. He looked up instead at the vast tree towering above him.

'Climb all the way to the top,' the tree whispered, 'and I will show you something beautiful that will stay with you for ever.'

Luca obeyed.

The forest watched.

Luca climbed slowly, feeling his way, dizzy with new sensations and only half-listening as the tree spoke to him of danger.

'Before the clock next chimes,' the tree said, 'you must make a choice.'

A ladybird crawled past. Luca thrust out a paw to catch it. The ladybird flew away.

'The choice cannot be undone,' said the tree.

If he wanted to catch bugs, thought Luca, he would have to be faster. He tensed his muscles, splayed his paws for a firmer grip and shot up the tree, using his tail to steady him. Light-headed with success, he left the trunk to run along a branch. On a branch close by, a beetle was crawling...

This time, Luca wasn't too slow. He gathered his paws, tensed, fixed his eyes on the beetle... pushed, leaped... stretched... flew!

Landed perfectly by the beetle, which he swept into his mouth in one swift movement, as if he had been doing it all his life.

It was delicious.

Luca forgot about reaching the top of the tree. Suddenly, all he could think about was food. He darted back to the trunk, climbing more slowly, stopping to look right, then left, sniffing the air – there! Tucked

between three interwoven
branches, a nest, and in the
nest, a clutch of pale blue
eggs... He hopped on to the
edge of the nest and, hanging
from his back feet, reached
inside...

'*Cahhh!*'

A small brown bird dive-bombed, aiming for
Luca's eyes. He swung upright and scrambled away,
skittered head-first to peer inside a
hollow, crawled in, sniffed – shot back
out, pursued by an owl.

Down he scurried, fearless.
He reached the forest floor
and his senses reeled, his nose
twitching at the scents of hart's
tongue and wild geranium, bracken
and wild garlic mingled with last
autumn's leaf fall, and beneath them
all the dark sweet-smelling earth. He
scampered over a pile of decaying
logs, touched noses with a snail,
played hopscotch over an anthill.

Until, little by little, this way
and that, he left the safety
of the big tree and came to
a grove of hazels, where a
new smell stopped him in his
tracks...

Mouth-watering, and close
beneath him...

Damp earth flew as Luca scrabbled at the ground,
but there was nothing here. He scrabbled again until
his paws connected with something hard – a nut,
plump and brown and luscious.

Luca sat back on his haunches, but no sooner
had he raised the nut to his mouth than...

'Run,' the big tree's voice floated to him from
far away.

Luca's fur prickled.

But the nut...

'RUN!'

Out of the branches of
a nearby ash a pine
marten pounced.

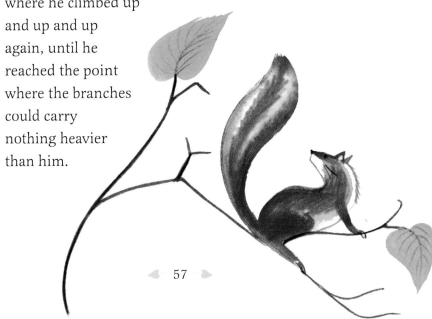

Luca caught a flash
of black and white, a
glimpse of fangs and claws.
For a fraction of a second, he
froze - then, dropping the nut, he ran.

Through the slim trunks of the hazel wood,
under the low hanging shoot of a holly... Into a gap
in the fallen branches of a dying spindle tree where
he froze, waiting for the pine marten to pass...

CRASH!

Luca ran on.

He zigzagged across the forest floor, back to the
pile of decaying logs and the trunk of the big tree
where he climbed up
and up and up
again, until he
reached the point
where the branches
could carry
nothing heavier
than him.

He was safe now and could have stopped. Yet still Luca climbed, drawn towards the top, higher and higher until twig tips bowed under his weight and there was...

The most beautiful thing he had ever seen.

Everywhere Luca looked, trees spread as far as the horizon. Oak and spiky pine, linden and silver birch, copper beeches and stately elm, all different, all woven together like a tapestry. Luca felt as if he was seeing the whole world, and that it went on for ever.

He lost his heart to it.

'Time is running out,' the tree murmured. 'You must choose. Will you stay as you are, or return to your other form?'

A choice? But between what? There was climbing and leaping, there was chasing and being chased, there was the heady scent of sap and the crunch of beetles, there was the feeling of flying with the world at your feet...

What else was there? What could be better than this?

Dimly Luca recalled the gentleness with which his mother had offered to show him her garden. He thought of how sick she had been and what it would do to her if he were to disappear.

He remembered his father, friends, games, meals...

And so he made his choice, and hurried to the ground. As the clock chimed, he became a boy again.

For the rest of his stay here, from morning till night, Luca explored the forest. He never regretted his choice, but when the time came to return to the city, though he carried us with him in his heart, a part of it remained here always.

There was silence for a while after the linden finished
its story.

'What Luca saw,' Olive said at last. 'The forest that
goes on for ever. I would like to see it.'

'There is time.'

'How much time?'

'Enough.'

'The thing is,' said Olive, 'if I saw it, I know that
I would love it too, like Luca
did. But I don't
know if I could
come back,
like he did.

And I can't do that, I mean go away for ever, because... well, of course, because my family would be upset but also because I made a promise.'

'Ah,' sighed the tree. 'A promise...'

'I'm sorry,' Olive said. 'I mean, if you're disappointed. I'm disappointed, to be honest. But the promise is important.'

'Perhaps,' the tree murmured, 'there is another way.'

Olive never forgot what happened next.

The linden shivered, and the branches before her parted like a curtain. For a short while, Olive saw what Luca had seen, the forest which went on for ever, and it was as vast and beautiful as she had hoped.

All too soon, the branches fell back.

'The promise I made,' she said. 'It was that one day I would speak out to protect trees.'

The linden swayed, listening.

'The forest,' said Olive. 'It doesn't stay like this. It gets... smaller.'

The linden sighed. 'But it can grow back.'

'Can it?'

'It's not so difficult for trees to grow, you know. We just need to be left alone.'

Olive stayed as long as she could on her perch at the top of the linden tree. When she heard the clock strike the hour, she climbed back down, hugged it (wrapping her arms around the trunk as far as they would go, which was not very far at all) then looked about her, hoping for a clue.

At the foot of the tree, laid like an offering in a circle of primroses, was a twig bearing the leaf and the unmistakeable catkins of an alder.

Olive picked it up. Somewhere downhill from the linden she could hear a river. Knowing something about alders, she headed towards it.

Unlike most woods, alder doesn't rot in water but gets stronger and harder.

There are about
35 species of alder –
they are a kind of birch tree.

They grow up to 28 metres tall.

They usually live to about
60 years old.

Alders are called pioneer trees because they are home to useful bacteria which fertilise the soil around them – over time alders will make the soil good enough for other trees to grow.

ALDER
Alnus

Alder

The river was fast and clear, green in colour, reflecting the surrounding trees. The bank was bright with pink and cream willowherb, the air smelled of clean wet earth and was full of birdsong and the sound of tumbling water. It was hard to imagine a prettier spot, but Olive had come here in search of alders – and the only ones she could see were on the other side of the river.

She crossed her arms and thought.

There was no bridge. She was going to have to wade across, but was it safe? There was only one way to find out.

Olive sat down and took off her shoes, tied the

laces together and hung them round her neck. Then
she rolled up her trousers as high as they would go
and waded into the water, wincing at the cold.

Mud squelched between her toes. She tried not to
think of what might be lurking in it. The mud gave
way to slippery boulders. Olive crouched, using her
hands to steady herself. The water rose steadily. Soon
it was up to her waist, pulling and tugging at her as it
rushed past.

This definitely wasn't safe. Olive glanced over
her shoulder. Should she go back? She had already
reached the middle of the river...

She went forward.

A few more steps, and the water level began to go
down. Olive let out her breath... and slipped.

She flailed, just managing to keep her head above water, trying to regain her footing, but the current was too strong and already she was being swept away. She tumbled over a boulder, briefly saw daylight, then sank deep into a dark pool.

Which way was up? Olive's lungs burned as she tried not to panic, reaching with toes and fingers to touch something, anything which might give her a clue.

Something brushed against her. For a brief moment – half a second – she thought she felt a hand take hers. Then, *whooosh*! She broke through the surface, gasping, and grabbed at a branch hanging over the water.

Clinging to the branch, Olive shuffled carefully

to the
bank where
she collapsed, shaking,
among the roots of an alder.

'Thank you,' she wheezed.

The alder's leaves pattered in the breeze. Olive looked up. The tree rose straight from the bank, the fissured bark of its trunk spotted with lichen, catkins hanging from its branches. She looked up to where the leaves on the canopy's twig tips brushed the sky, then down to where the roots reached into the water.

'I felt a hand,' she croaked. 'I'm sure I did. Was it you?'

'Maybe, maybe not.' The alder's voice was airy and watery at once, completely unlike the oak and the linden. 'There are many strange things in the water. Did you feel the river as you came across? How it pulls and pushes?'

'I did,' said Olive, nodding hard.

'All the way to the ocean,' the alder murmured. 'Did you know that in the ocean there are whole forests underwater? I dream of them sometimes. They are made of kelp.'

The alder rolled the word kelp as Olive might roll a toffee on her tongue.

Olive's teeth began to chatter.

'Come away from the water,' the alder said. 'It's warmer on the riverbank. Dry yourself, and when you are ready I will tell you about them.'

Olive climbed out of the water. She found a sheltered spot facing the sun, wrung out her T-shirt and trousers, hung her shoes from a branch to drip and took the bands out of her hair, then she jumped about a bit. When she was quite warmed up, she snuggled into a mossy hollow among the alder's roots.

'I'm ready.'

'Then I will begin.'

'ONCE UPON A TIME,'
said the alder, 'there
was a mermaid.'
'A mermaid?'
This was not what
Olive had been
expecting.
'Her name
was Salt,' the alder
continued, 'and
her best friend was a
merboy called Brine.
The two of them had shared
a shell as babies – you know, I'm sure, that
shells are what merrows use for cradles – and they
had been devoted to each other ever since. At the time
of our story they were a hundred and ten in mermaid
years, which means they were eleven in human years,
about the size of a dolphin, with sharp mermaid
fangs for chewing shellfish and beautiful long hair.

That hair! Red and brown and green and gold, it
flowed from their blue human-shaped heads all along
their blue human-shaped bodies right to the end of
their silver blue fish tails, and it was their absolute

pride. Salt wore hers loose, rarely tending it, enjoying the snacks which got caught in its tangles – shrimp and baby crabs and so on. Brine, on the other hand, looked after his. Salt laughed at him for it, but he didn't care. He spent hours grooming every day, and his locks floated about him like a well-conditioned cloud.

These young merrows were wild. All merrows like to explore but Salt and Brine were unstoppable, and they went everywhere together.

It didn't matter what rules their teachers and
families set – be home by moonrise, don't tease the
giant octopus, don't swim into unknown wrecks.
Salt and Brine ignored them all. From the moment
the morning light pierced the waves, they plunged
out of their cave and into the open ocean. And who
can blame them? Can you imagine the joy of it?
A whole ocean for a playground, with your best
friend by your side...

All day, Salt and Brine would swim for miles and miles, often staying out long after the sun set and the moon and stars came out. Over reefs and into caves, through shipwrecks and canyons, so fast sometimes they appeared no more than a silver shimmer, their hair streaming behind them. When they grew hungry, they used the razor-clam knives every merrow carries to prise shellfish from rocks. When they grew sleepy, they napped in beds of seagrass or anemones.

Now mermaids, as you know, are friends of all the creatures in the ocean. They really only have one predator, and I do not mean walruses. It is true that walruses and mermaids don't always get along, but that has nothing to do with this story and anyway, walruses live in very cold places where mermaids hardly ever go. The predator I refer to is the Human Being.'

The alder paused.

'What?' protested Olive. 'I would never hurt a mermaid!'

'The Human Being,' the alder resumed. 'Especially, the Human Being Who Goes to Sea. Even more especially, the Human Being Who Goes to Sea in Fishing Boats.

For centuries there was little danger. Fishing boats were small. Humans, for the most part, were respectful. They took what they needed, mermaids did the same, and there was a balance in the oceans which everyone was happy with, even the fish.

But something was happening to the humans. There were more and more of them, and they were growing clever. As their numbers and cleverness grew, so did their boats, until the little wooden craft of old were replaced by much bigger ships which trawled nets through the ocean from which nothing could escape.

The mermaids changed their ways. When the shadow of a trawler appeared they dived deep, hiding in underwater caves out of reach of the nets. It was hard, especially for adventurous young merrows used to swimming and exploring, but they had to, not only to protect themselves but for the sake of merrows everywhere. Who knew what would happen, if even one merrow was caught? At best, they would be put in a tank for humans to look at. At worst, the fisherfolk would come hunting for more until there were none left.

It is what humans do.

And so the merrows hid and made the best of it. They decorated their deepwater caves with seaweed and anemones, they made board games from coral and pearls, they brushed each other's hair and held exercise classes and made up songs and plays. Salt and Brine – who were well-meaning, even if they weren't always good – did as they were told and hardly complained.

Until there came a terrible time when for day after day the trawlers never went away.

Salt and Brine tried. They really did. For five days they played board games and listened to stories and joined in the singing, but on the sixth day it became too much.

'I'm not sure if I even know how to swim any more,' groaned Brine.

Salt gave her tail an experimental *swooosh*.

'It still works,' she said. 'But if I stay here any longer it's going to fall off.'

'We might turn into lobsters,' said Brine, and
they both pulled faces because though, of course, all
sea creatures were their friends, what fun was it to
always crawl along the ocean floor?

They bobbed together to the mouth of the cave and
gazed out. The ocean stretched before them, a deep
cobalt blue. They peered up.

There were the trawlers, terrible dark shadows.

'We could go a little way,' said Salt. 'As long as it's not towards the boats.'

'Just to make sure we can still swim,' said Brine.

And, when no one was looking, they slipped out of the cave.

When you start doing something you love after ages of being told you can't, it is almost impossible to stop.

It started with another *swooosh* to shake out the cramp of a week without swimming... then a bigger

swish ... and they were off!

Salt and Brine shot through the water like silver arrows, leaving a cloud of bubbles behind them. Up to the surface to see the lovely sun, down to the canyons to slalom through the coral, diving, chasing, pirouetting until they lost their bearings, faster and faster and faster...

Salt saw the net and swerved just in time.

Brine was not so lucky.

He tried to turn back, but there were already hundreds of fish in the net, and they were panicking.

'Salt!' he cried. 'Help me!'

'I'm trying!' Her answer floated back to him through the tightly packed fish. Brine could tell from her voice that she was panicking too. She was trying, trying hard, sawing at the net with her little knife, but a knife made from a razor clam stands no chance against the tough fibres of a net.

CRUNCH! CLANK! CLUNK!

What was happening? The net was growing tighter, pulling in. Crushed among the fishes, Brine struggled to breathe. Salt looked towards the surface and felt her cold mermaid blood grow colder still.

The net was being slowly winched out of the water.

With a strangled sob, Salt shoved her knife back into its pouch, seized the net with her hands and started to gnaw at the mesh with her fangs.

CRUNCH! CLANK! CLUNK!

went the big boat's winch, and up, up, up went the two little merrows and the hundreds of fishes, and all the time Salt gnawed and nibbled and tried not to cry until suddenly, a strand in the mesh broke. No time to rest though, because the gap was narrow. Gnaw, gnaw, gnaw until her jaw was burning. Another strand broke, then another. Salt pulled the net open, scooped out one terrified fish and then another, until the rest understood and began to stream past her until at last there was only Brine left squeezing through the hole, his head, his blue shoulders, his...

'Ow!'

Brine's beautiful hair was wound tight and fast in the net. Salt tugged at it, but it was no use. The more she tugged, the more knotted it became.

And the net continued to rise.

There was only one thing to do.

She drew her knife again.

Brine whimpered and raised his hands to stop her. Salt pushed them aside.

'You have to let me do this,' she said.

Any second now, the net would break the surface and Brine would be caught.

Salt would lose her best friend.

Humans would know about merrows...

There was no time to lose.

With a few determined strokes of her little knife, Salt sliced through Brine's beautiful hair. As the top of the net broke through the waves, she took his hands. She helped him ease out his blue human-shaped body, his silver blue fish tail and she pulled him away and down until they reached the safety of a wreck.

'My hair!' Brine wept. 'My beautiful hair!'

Salt did not laugh at him, as she might have. Nor did she point out that by cutting his hair, she had saved his life. Instead, she took a long strand of her own tangled locks in one hand, and with the other she raised her knife.

SLASH.

She didn't stop until all her hair was cut.

'There!' She ran her hands over her scalp. 'A new fashion!'

Exhausted, bald and very relieved, the little
merrows swam home to a scolding, cries of horror,
an enormous bowl of whelks and bed.

But let's not forget the underwater forest.

For days, Salt and Brine's long merrow locks
floated on the currents, until they washed into
shallow coastal waters and sank to the ocean floor
where they took root. Once rooted, they began to

grow, fast and strong, green and red and brown and gold, reaching up towards the light until in some places they grew as tall as an oak. They spread and spread to almost a quarter of the world's coasts, growing stronger and tougher until they formed a forest which fish used as nurseries for their young, and where seabirds and sea lions, otters and even whales sheltered from predators and storms.

The alder sighed.

'Isn't that a beautiful story?'

'It is.' Olive licked her lips, and thought she tasted salt. 'Is it true?'

'Oh, quite true,' the alder assured her. 'I heard it from a seagull.'

Olive remembered the last time she had been to the seaside. An enormous herring gull had stolen her chips. *Gulls*, thought Olive, *were not exactly to be trusted.*

The clock in the tower struck the hour. The alder's leaves pattered. Olive sat a little longer, thinking about Salt and Brine as she watched the pushing pulling river rush towards the ocean.

When she got home, she decided, she would find out everything she could about kelp forests.

Her clothes and hair were not as dry as she would have liked, and her shoes were still wet. She made a face as she pulled the first one on, then squeaked as her foot pushed against something hard and prickly. She upended the shoe and shook it. The fruit of a plane tree tumbled out.

A narrow path led from the river at the foot of the alder into the woods, with a trail of other plane fruits strewn along it, showing her the way. Olive pulled on her wet shoes and followed them.

As she walked, she licked her lips again.

They did taste of salt.

Planes are one of the best air-cleaning trees, and are planted in cities worldwide.

There are about 10 species of plane tree.

They normally grow 30-50 metres tall.

They live for several hundred years.

The London plane is a cross between two trees from opposite sides of the world: the American sycamore and the Oriental plane.

LONDON PLANE

Platanus x hispanica

Plane

The path led Olive through a wood of silver birch, glinting and shimmering in the midday sun, with bluebells beginning to unfurl across the forest floor. It felt wild and magical, but Olive was tired.

What a day she had had! The oak tree, the hunt, the giant linden, her tumble in the river! The promise she had made the forest...

She needed to rest.

After walking a while, she stopped at a fork in the path. The main fork carried on into the trees. The other led to a gate in a wall.

Which way should she go?

Olive looked along the path, and saw that it
narrowed, and that the woods grew darker. She
turned her gaze to the gate: the park beyond was
bright with sunlight, and somewhere in that sunlight
a blackbird called to her.

Still Olive hesitated, because though she longed
for the warm sun she loved the wild forest and didn't
want to leave it. But she was so tired, and so cold too
because of her damp clothes...

The blackbird called again.

Olive went through the gate.

For a moment, she was confused. She knew exactly where she was, in an unremarkable corner of the park where no one ever came. But it looked different today. Restful. A well-raked path wound through flowering shrubs to a circular lawn, in the centre of which stood a plane tree she had never noticed before, with wide leaves on delicate stems, clusters of round fruit like the one she had found in her shoe, and a mottled grey trunk.

It was not a remarkable tree like the oak and
the linden or even the alder. It was simply inviting.
'Come!' the tree seemed to say, through the gracious
rustle of its leaves. 'Sit close, and rest.'

Olive did as she was told. She took off her damp
shoes and lay down, not in full sun but in light
delicious shade where she grew the exact right
amount of warmer, and gazed at the bright blue sky
through the gently swaying branches, and felt her
tiredness slip away.

'It's time for the fourth story,' said the tree.

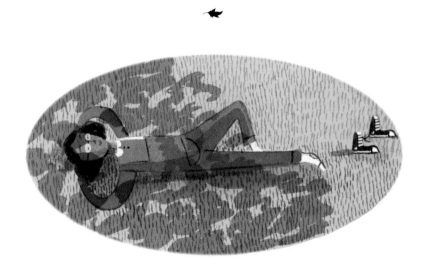

❧ ONCE UPON A TIME, at the heart of a rich and powerful city, there was a garden. It was a public garden – a park – with benches to sit on, a duck pond with a fountain in the middle and a kiosk selling tea and pastries stuffed with nuts and honey. There was a rose garden, a herb garden, a formal garden, and there were trees – many trees! Purple flowering jacaranda and sweet-scented oleander, dark cypresses and towering pines.

And plane trees.

There were thousands of us in the city, cleaning the dirty air, filling it with our fragrance in the spring, spreading cool shade over the pavements in summer. Perhaps it sounds boastful, but the city would have been poorer without us. Yet people hardly noticed us. We were as common a part of the city as the buildings or the pigeons.

Except for one tree.

For decades this tree grew in the middle of the public garden, as tall and fine and unnoticed as the others in the city, but in its thirtieth summer a lightning bolt burned it to a stump.

Through the long hot days that followed, the park gardeners argued about what they should do with this stump. Some called it ugly and said it should be removed. Others wanted to keep it, dead wood being a good place for grubs and insects, and so for birds and other wildlife.

Winter came before they could agree, bringing months of snow. When spring returned, a decision was made: the stump would go. But as the first woodcutter's saw bit into its sad remains, a girl who had stopped to watch with her mother shouted, 'Mama, Mama! I can see green!' The woodcutter put down his saw and

looked more closely. Sure enough, out of the wood everyone had thought was dead, a green shoot was beginning to grow.

'A miracle,' said the woodcutter, and the gardeners who had gathered to help him bowed their heads in respect.

Of course, it was not a miracle. Growing is simply what trees do: as long as some part of us is alive, we will find a way. And so over the years, the tree grew, but it was never truly graceful again. Its once slender

trunk was squat and thick with nodes, its new limbs comically thin compared to its heavy body. But in time its branches grew generous and wide, and people loved it. It was known as the tree of hope.

Small wonder then that the storyteller chose it.

Nobody remembered exactly when the storyteller came to the garden. One day, no one had ever heard of her. Next morning she was just there, an old woman with a face as wrinkled as the bark of the tree itself and silver hair which floated on the breeze like leaves.

From the day she arrived, the storyteller followed the same routine.

As soon as the park opened, she spread a blanket beneath the tree. Then she stood on the blanket in her bare feet and touched her toes twelve times. Then, out of a covered basket, she took a flask and a honey cake. She nibbled the cake until it was all gone and drank two cups of strong, black coffee. She ignored anyone who tried to talk to her.

Breakfast was a serious affair.

After she
had packed
away her
flask and cup,
the storyteller laid
her hands on the tree
and wished it a good morning.
Then she opened for business.

First came old people, asking for stories
about being young. The storyteller spun tales
about dancing and moonlight and falling in
love, and as she spoke the listeners felt new life
stirring in their bones, just as the tree did after
the lightning strike.

Next came young mothers with their
babies, and the storyteller would sing
soft songs which the wind would
echo in the leaves and branches
of the tree, and the little ones
cooed and gurgled while their
exhausted mothers rested.

At lunchtime,
office workers
came to hear
tales of holidays
and faraway places. And in the afternoons,
when school children came, the story requests
grew wild.

'Tell us about a goat
who eats nothing but
bananas!' they might ask.
'Tell us about a cockroach
in a hot air balloon!' The
storyteller could reduce
a class to giggles with her
tales. But once, when the

rest of his classmates had
gone, a boy stayed behind
and in a small voice asked
for a story about a bully
who stole people's
lunchboxes.

The storyteller and the boy sat together on her blanket as a blackbird sang above them, and she told him a story of courage and friendship. When she had finished the boy hugged the tree and left for home with a skip in his step, feeling brave.

So it was in the garden, under the tree of hope. The storyteller never took money, but she accepted gifts of food and drink which she shared with those who needed it. Sometimes children brought her drawings which together, if she was feeling playful, they turned into boats to float on the pond, as she told them tales of shipwrecks and desert islands.

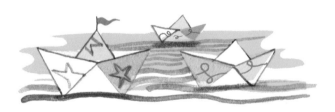

Now, at that time the city was ruled by a duchess, who was not in the least interested in stories or lightning trees or paper boats. What the duchess wanted was to make the city more powerful and wealthy than it already was, and because of this she wanted to start a war. The state which neighboured the city had forests that she could cut down for buildings and diamond mines in its mountains that she could plunder. It was even said that its rivers were flecked with gold.

The duchess's plan was to force all the young people in the city to become soldiers. With these new soldiers and her existing army, she would invade the neighbouring state. It would be a quick war, easily won!

In the springtime when this story happens, as children and babies and elderly citizens gathered beneath the tree of hope to listen to the storyteller, the new

soldiers were marching daily up and down the parade
grounds of the duchess's palace, and the city streets
rang to the sound of their boots. War was coming.
Some people thought it would make them richer, but
many more were afraid. They knew that war only
ever benefits a few, and means hardship and sorrow
for most. In the bars and taverns, in houses and
parks, citizens began to mutter against the duchess.

They said that she was not a good ruler.

They said that she should be replaced by someone who did not want a war.

The duchess was furious when news of this reached her. Some of her younger ministers – those who thought war would make them richer – said she should arrest everyone who spoke against her. But an older, wiser minister knew better.

'You must make people love you,' he said.

'How?' demanded the duchess.

'You must go to the garden at the heart of the city and ask the storyteller who sits beneath the tree of hope to tell a story about you. A great story, celebrating how rich and beautiful the city will be, once the war is won.'

The duchess was unsure. As I said, she wasn't interested in stories or trees. But the minister insisted, and so she sent him to the garden to order the storyteller to write her a story.

'Well?' she demanded, when the minister returned.

'I'm afraid the storyteller said no,' he replied. 'She said, she does not write stories, she tells them. And she does not like war.'

'How absolutely ridiculous,' said the duchess. And she sent him again, with six tall guards carrying sharp spears and swords to frighten the storyteller.

This time the minister arrived at breakfast time. He waited respectfully as the storyteller did her morning stretches and poured her coffee and nibbled her honey cakes. But again, when he asked, the storyteller said no.

'She says, if you wish for a story from her, you must go to the garden yourself and sit beneath the tree of hope, and hear it with your own ears.'

'Even more ridiculous!' cried the duchess. 'Me, in a public garden! Under a tree! The very idea!'

'I'm afraid she insisted,' said the minister.

And so the duchess went.

She arrived at the garden in a gold-plated carriage drawn by four grey horses. She was dressed in robes of silk with velvet slippers on her feet, and accompanied by

bodyguards in black, red and gold. For a moment, she felt unsettled. She had imagined the storyteller would be a fine-looking person, serious and superior, lost in thought. She had not expected a plump old woman with long silver hair surrounded by hordes of children, all howling with laughter at a story about a mouse, a cook and a pot of raspberry jam.

The children stopped laughing when they saw the duchess and her bodyguards. They turned to the storyteller, wondering if they ought to go, but she gestured at them to stay.

'Your Grace,' she murmured, bowing her head to the duchess. 'To what do I owe the honour?'

The duchess wanted to spit that the storyteller knew very well to what she owed the honour, but her minister had advised her to be patient.

'I wish for a story,' she declared. 'A great story, celebrating the future riches of our city.'

The storyteller said, 'I'm afraid that's not how this works.'

'I will pay you,' the duchess coaxed. 'Name your price. Do you want gold, diamonds, jewels?'

'What use have I for jewels?' asked the storyteller with a smile.

'If you don't obey me,' the duchess snarled, 'I will
have you thrown in jail!'

The children looked fearfully at the storyteller. She
had told them a story once about the city jail. It was a
terrible place, with walls that dripped slime and rats
that ate your toes while you slept. She couldn't go
to jail! But they knew that she was against the war –
surely she couldn't tell a story defending it?

For a while, the storyteller remained silent, her
brow furrowed in thought. At last she looked up and
nodded.

'Very well,' she said.
'You shall have your
story, and it shall
celebrate the
future riches
of the city.'

Some of the children were disappointed because
they thought the storyteller should have resisted.
Others were relieved because they didn't want her to
go to jail. As they huddled on the grass waiting for
the story to begin, their minds filled with different
images. Some saw soldiers and marching bands,
others battles and bloodshed. The boy who had
asked for the story about the bully and the lunchbox
wondered whether he would be brave enough to
defend the storyteller if the guards tried to take her
away. The duchess wondered if, when the war was
won, she might order a statue of herself to be put up
in the park.

Her guards mainly thought of beer.

Cross-legged on her blanket, the storyteller closed
her eyes.

And they waited.

And waited.

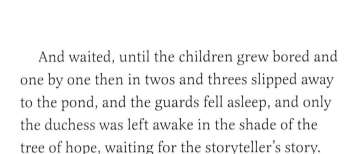

And waited, until the children grew bored and one by one then in twos and threes slipped away to the pond, and the guards fell asleep, and only the duchess was left awake in the shade of the tree of hope, waiting for the storyteller's story.

The storyteller did not speak.

The duchess wanted to shake the stubborn old woman who sat before her so peacefully. But from the corner of her eye she spotted a boy clutching a lunchbox and glaring at her. She decided it wouldn't look good for her to attack the old woman. The duchess groaned and, leaning back on her elbows, looked up at the branches of the lightning tree, the tree of hope.

How long it had been, since she'd done this – lain on the grass in a garden, looking up at a tree! Through the delicate long-fingered branches of the plane tree, she saw that the sky was a deep bright blue – the colour of summer on its way.

The spring breeze was warm and scented; it smelled of flowers, and warm earth, and pastry from the tea kiosk. Suddenly, she remembered the cakes her grandmother used to buy for her as a child – tasted the hazelnuts and almonds, the honey, the crackling buttery pastry. Vaguely, she thought of sending the child to buy her some, but he was lying on his back now too, gazing at the tree. What was he looking at? The duchess shifted and saw in the leaves a small bird. Her heart leaped – a blackbird!

When had she last listened to a blackbird?

She watched it anxiously, hoping it would sing, and she closed her eyes to listen when it did.

It was a love song, the duchess remembered.

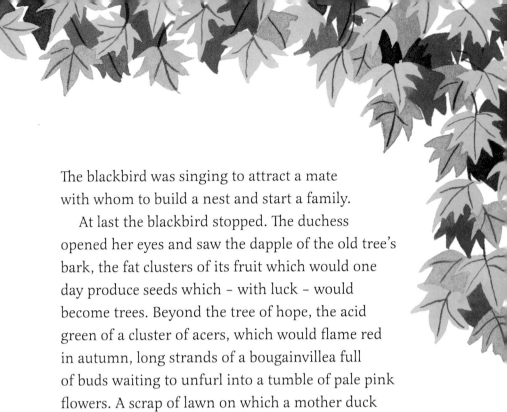

The blackbird was singing to attract a mate
with whom to build a nest and start a family.

At last the blackbird stopped. The duchess
opened her eyes and saw the dapple of the old tree's
bark, the fat clusters of its fruit which would one
day produce seeds which – with luck – would
become trees. Beyond the tree of hope, the acid
green of a cluster of acers, which would flame red
in autumn, long strands of a bougainvillea full
of buds waiting to unfurl into a tumble of pale pink
flowers. A scrap of lawn on which a mother duck
paraded her ducklings. From the pond, she heard
the calls and laughter of children.

The duchess sighed, and it
was another happy sound to add to
the many in the garden that afternoon.
The storyteller opened her eyes.

'You enjoyed your story,' she observed.

'My story?' The duchess was puzzled.

'You asked for a story about the future riches of
the city.'

'I...' For a moment, the duchess was confused, but
then she understood. The children, the ducklings, the
flower buds, the seeds – all were a promise of what
was to come. And she understood then that it was not
necessary to go to war for the city to be rich. It was
already rich enough.

'You tricked me,' she told the storyteller. 'I should
throw you in jail.'

'It was not a trick,' the storyteller said. 'I showed
you how to listen.'

And then, after a respectful bow, she went to
find the children at the pond.

For a few seconds, the duchess considered
joining them. But floating paper
boats on ponds is not something
duchesses do, however much

they want to. She did allow herself one pleasure though: before she stepped back into her carriage, she sent one of her guards to the kiosk, to buy her a honey cake...

And the city did not go to war.

'Because the duchess sat under a tree?' Olive was impressed.

'Because the tree granted her wisdom,' said the plane tree. 'Because she paid attention. Because she realised the value of what she already had, and the madness of killing many people – and incidentally, many trees – in order to become richer than she needed to be. She learned to appreciate what she already had.'

Olive thought about this.

'The way I appreciate my oak tree,' she said. 'But my father is like the duchess.'

'Many people are like the duchess,' said the plane tree.

'I have another question,' said Olive. 'When you were talking about the city trees, it sounded as if you were there. Were you? I don't see how you can have been.'

'Possibly,' the tree said, 'the seed was there which bore the tree which bore the seed which became me, and that is how

I know the story. One way or another, we are all connected.'

'Like the mermaids and the kelp,' said Olive. 'And the big oak and the little oak.'

But already the clock tower was sounding the fourth hour, and the tree's only response was a gentle rising and falling of leaves in the breeze. Olive stood and stretched, feeling perfectly refreshed. Reaching for her shoes, she found that they were dry.

The plane tree had looked after her well.

A hint of pink in the grass caught her eye. She walked to it and picked it up. It was a sprig of apple blossom. Olive smiled and set off towards the orchard.

The wild apple trees from the mountain forests of eastern Kazakhstan are the ancestors of all the apples we eat.

There are between
30 and 55 species of
wild apple tree.

They grow
5-12 metres tall.

They live 80-100 years.

There are over seven and a half thousand sorts of eating apples, but not all are sold in shops!

WILD APPLE
Malus

Wild Apple

he apple orchard stood behind high walls, designed to keep out thieves and predators. Inside those walls were thirteen trees, different sorts with wonderful names like Grenadier and Northern Spy and Opal – apples for eating and cooking, apples for juicing, apples for making jelly, apples which the gardener said were no good for people but which the honeybees from the nearby hives loved. It was like a different world behind those high walls. When she was younger, before she had discovered her oak, this had been Olive's favourite place to come and read and play. In autumn, when the trees' branches were weighed down with fruit, she pretended the apples

were precious
jewels. In spring, when
the trees flowered, she called
it fairyland.

As she approached the orchard
from the plane tree, Olive smelled the
apples before she saw them. Their scent
wafted over the walls in breezy puffs,
bringing to mind pies and tarts, picnics and
autumn bonfires. Olive sniffed the air happily
and opened the door.

Clouds of flowers greeted her, from deepest
pink to a crisp white that was almost green.
Listening carefully, beneath the breeze and the
birdsong, she heard the buzz of tiny wings.

Olive smiled.

Fairyland.

Then the voices started. And they were
distinctly unfairy-like.

'Someone's coming! I can hear footsteps! Who is it? Ooh, I'm so nervous I might drop my blossom!'

'It's the little human! We haven't seen her for a while.'

'I hope she doesn't try to climb us. She's bigger than she was.'

'She's wearing very strange clothes,' another voice remarked. 'Like a dress, but trousers. And what's she done to her hair?'

Should she say something? Sometimes, when Nana asked Olive to help with tea when her friends visited, the old ladies talked about her as if she wasn't there. Olive wanted to tell them to stop, but never dared.

This was different though – wasn't it?

Olive cleared her throat for courage.

'You do know I can hear you?'

The voices fell quiet. A few blossoms fluttered off a flustered Pink Lady.

'I just thought you should know,' Olive said.

Still silence. What should she say now?

'Please will you tell me how you came to be so pretty?'

All around the orchard, blossom quivered as the apple trees began to chatter.

'A delightful little human!'

'A perfect Pippin!'

'I rather like her hair.'

'Apples, please!' The new voice was lower and huskier than the rest. It came from an ancient Egremont Russet, its trunk splendidly gnarled, its branches heavy with blossom. 'The little human asked a question. As the most ancient tree in this orchard – the founding tree, for I was here when most of you were pips – I will answer.'

Olive beamed with relief. She found a comfortable place to sit on a mossy tussock in the shade of a Worcester Pearmain, and the Egremont began.

ꙮ ONCE
THERE WERE
THREE SISTERS,
born in three
successive springs:
Willow first, then Rowan,
and Hazel last of all. They
lived in a land far from here, in an old stone house in
a village high in the mountains, where summers were
hot and bright and winter snows cut off the outside
world for months.

Their early years were happy. Their parents were
merchants and though they were not rich, they
wanted for nothing. Most importantly, they adored
their daughters. Their papa taught them to ride. Their
mama taught them the names of every flower in the
meadows, like lupins and campanula and orchids.
But one winter, when the girls were only young, both
parents grew sick and died.

'Always look after each other,' were their mother's last words to her daughters, and they promised that it would be so.

The girls' uncle and aunt came to the house in the mountains to care for them and to take over the business.

Now, the sisters did not have a bad life. Their uncle and aunt did not love them, but they never went hungry like unloved children in fairy tales. They had a big room to themselves at the top of the house, with comfortable beds and warm blankets. They had good clothes, and went to school, and had friends. Best of all, they had the sturdy mountain ponies on which Papa had taught them to ride. Every day after school, they rushed through their chores to ride up into the mountains.

Sometimes, at night, they would talk about their parents, the way Papa gathered his three girls in his arms at once, or Mama's songs as she tended her garden. But as long as they had their freedom and each other, they were happy.

Their uncle, however, had plans.

What the uncle wanted, more than anything, was to be rich. He traded far and wide beyond the mountains, even beyond the sea, which the girls had never seen, but it was not enough for him.

He decided that as soon as Hazel was old enough, he would marry them off to the sons of the people he traded with most, so their riches would be his too. The sisters would be separated, with whole oceans and continents between them, but that didn't matter one bit to their uncle.

The sisters knew nothing of their uncle's plan until the day of Hazel's sixteenth birthday. Willow and Rowan had planned a beautiful day. They were going to ride up to a high rock where a pair of eagles had made their nest and they hoped that, with care and patience, they might see the eaglets. Afterwards they were going to have a picnic. But as they prepared their ponies in the stables, their aunt marched out of the house and swept them back indoors.

'It's Hazel's birthday though!'
Rowan protested.

'No time for that!' snapped the aunt.
'We must PREPARE.'

Hazel, who had been looking forward to her
birthday, went pink as she always did when she
was about to cry. Willow put an arm around her and
asked, 'Prepare for what?'

Their aunt explained her husband's plans.

'Your uncle has ordered the finest cloth from town
to make your wedding clothes,' she said, ignoring
the sisters' bewildered looks. 'When they are ready,
we will go to the city in the valley where you will be
married all at once before going your separate ways.'

The sisters were horrified. They followed their aunt
into the dining room and saw, draped over the table,
the reams of rich brocade their uncle had chosen,
ready to be cut and sewed into their wedding
clothes.

'Your uncle wants you looking splendid for
the occasion. Isn't that nice?'

As if pretty dresses could make up
for lost sisters! Hazel began to weep,
then Rowan. But Willow waited

until their aunt had left, then put down her cutting scissors and drew her sisters close.

'Stop crying and listen!' she said. 'We are to be married when our clothes are ready. What we must do is work very, very slowly, until summer passes and the snows return and the village is once again cut off. Then our bridegrooms will go away, and we can stay together.'

Rowan sniffed. 'What if they return in the spring?'

'Do you have a better plan?' asked Willow.

Rowan admitted that she did not.

'Can't we run away?' Hazel tried to keep the tremble out of her voice. 'Wouldn't that be better?'

'They'd only catch us,' said Willow.

And so it was agreed.

For the next two weeks, the sisters worked as slowly as they dared. The weather was on their side, mild and fair, and their aunt was busy in her garden. But at the beginning of the third week, it began to rain. Their aunt came in to sit with her nieces and saw how their needles crept over their sewing, where in normal times they flew.

'Anyone would think you don't want to be married,' she said.

'Oh, no, Aunt!' Hazel could look very innocent when she wanted to. 'We are only taking extra care to make our clothes perfect.'

'Hmm,' said their aunt. 'Even so, from now on I will stay and watch.'

'I will unpick the stitches when our aunt is sleeping,' Willow said when the sisters were in their bedroom.

And every night for a week, when the house was quiet, she tiptoed downstairs to the dining room and unpicked the day's work.

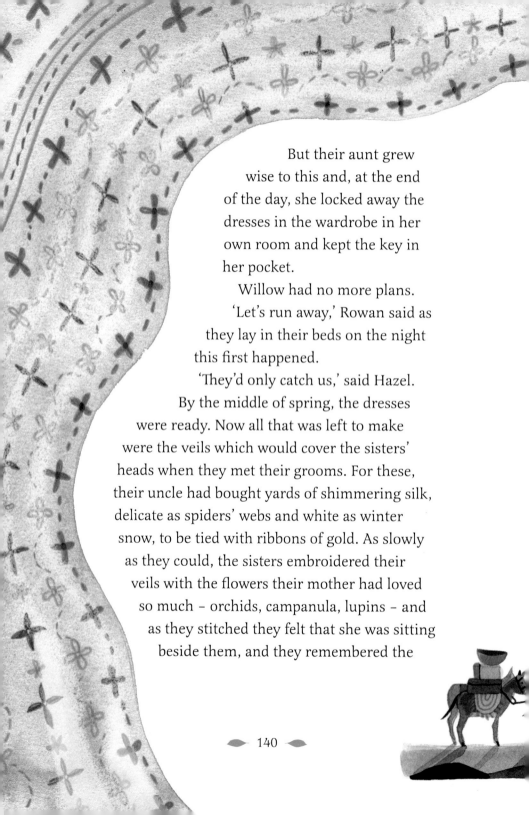

But their aunt grew
wise to this and, at the end
of the day, she locked away the
dresses in the wardrobe in her
own room and kept the key in
her pocket.

Willow had no more plans.

'Let's run away,' Rowan said as
they lay in their beds on the night
this first happened.

'They'd only catch us,' said Hazel.

By the middle of spring, the dresses
were ready. Now all that was left to make
were the veils which would cover the sisters'
heads when they met their grooms. For these,
their uncle had bought yards of shimmering silk,
delicate as spiders' webs and white as winter
snow, to be tied with ribbons of gold. As slowly
as they could, the sisters embroidered their
veils with the flowers their mother had loved
so much – orchids, campanula, lupins – and
as they stitched they felt that she was sitting
beside them, and they remembered the

promise they had made to her so many years ago, to always look after each other.

'We will find each other again,' they said. 'Wherever we are in the world, we will find each other.'

They wept so hard they pricked their fingers, and blood dripped on to the fabric.

At last – too soon – the veils were ready.

The city where the wedding was to take place was two days away on horseback. Off they set, the sisters on their ponies, the uncle and aunt and a groom riding bigger horses, a servant on a mule leading two donkeys carrying the luggage. Up they climbed away from the only home they had ever known, past the wildflower meadows and the summer lakes, through the summer pastures where cows grazed with bells around their necks, past the rocky outcrop where they had hoped to see the eagles' nest, to the pass which led out of their mountain.

This was the edge of what they knew.

There was no going back.

One by one, the girls rode through the hostile granite pass to the other side.

'Goodness,' breathed Willow, the first to emerge, and, 'Goodness,' Rowan then Hazel agreed.

Spread before them, they saw a chain of mountains and valleys, tapering to hills and fields, a glittering city and beyond that a line of blue which was the sea.

'I did not know,' Rowan said, 'that the world would be so big.'

They did not speak more of what they had seen. But that night, as they lay in their tent on the edge of a forest, Hazel reached for her sisters' hands and they knew that they were thinking the same thing.

Late in the afternoon of the second day, they entered the city's valley.

It was wide and flat, with a river and a road running through it, and rich pastures with gentle slopes on either side where wild apple trees grew.

Remember that, please. It's important.

The following afternoon, after another day of riding, the uncle gave the signal to stop by a stream, and they dismounted. Behind a sheet held up as a screen, the sisters stripped off their riding clothes and washed, then braided each other's hair. When at last they could put it off no longer, they helped each other dress.

On went the gowns of rich brocade.

On went the blood-spattered, flower-embroidered veils, the ribbons of gold.

'Ready?' asked Willow.

'Ready,' whispered Rowan and Hazel.

They lowered their veils.

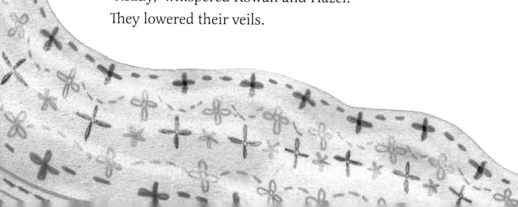

The sisters returned to their waiting uncle and aunt. The servant raised a horn to his lips.

Three short blasts.

'We are here!' cried the horn. 'The brides approach!'

From the far end of the valley came three answering notes of a trumpet.

'We are here!' cried the trumpet. 'The bridegrooms await!'

There was music now at the far end of the valley. More trumpets, pipes, the long clear note of a horn.

Hazel raised her veil, saw fluttering flags and people on horseback. Her aunt frowned at her. She lowered the veil.

'They're coming to meet us,' she said.

Willow reached for her sisters' hands and squeezed them.

Rowan and Hazel squeezed back.

'Back in the saddle, everyone!' ordered the uncle. 'We will ride to meet them.'

Their hearts in their mouths, the sisters climbed back on to their tough mountain ponies. Hazel's hands trembled and Rowan's legs shook, but Willow sat straight and calm. She waited until she was sure that everyone's attention was fixed on the approaching party...

... and nodded.

As one, the sisters wheeled their ponies and kicked them into a gallop. Hard and fast as they could they went, straight up the side of the mountain among the apple trees, their wedding dresses streaming behind them, their veils lifting away from their faces.

Hazel glanced over her shoulder. The uncle and the groom were already after them, galloping hell for leather on their bigger horses.

'They're catching up!' she yelled.

'Ride faster!' Rowan yelled back.

But Hazel's pony was the smallest of the three, and already going as fast as he could. She could hear the hooves of the horses gaining on her, she could hear her uncle shouting...

With a howl of rage and defiance, she ripped her veil from her head and flung it behind her.

And the strangest thing happened.

The veil caught the breeze and began to float. Like a bird, it floated, or a sail, and as it floated it grew... wider and wider, impossibly wide, until it covered the whole valley like a mist. Hazel cried for her sisters to look. Seeing what had happened, they also ripped off their veils and these too stretched over the valley. The mist turned to fog. Lost inside it, their uncle cursed. Up in the clear air above, the sisters watched a while in wonder, then galloped away.

For all I know, they are galloping still, all over the big wide world.

Their uncle, the groom, the search party which came looking for them, their aunt, the servant and several locals remained trapped in the fog for two days and two nights.

But when the sun rose on the third day, they saw that the lovely flowers the sisters had stitched into their veils in memory of their mother were settling on the trees. Some were pure white. Others, touched with the sisters' blood, were different shades of pink. At the heart of each flower, bees were already feeding on strands of golden pollen, the colour of the ribbons which had held the veils to the brides' heads.

It was a miracle. And the most miraculous thing was that every year it happened again. Apple blossom flowered over the wild hillsides and people came from far and wide to admire it.

And that, little human, is how we became so pretty.

Drifts of apple blossom wafted through the orchard as the trees let out contented sighs.

And the clock in the tower struck for the fifth time.

Olive lingered, thinking about mountains covered in flowering apple trees, and wedding veils embroidered with promises and love, and sisters galloping through the wide, wide world. But then she looked up at the blossom above her, buzzing with bees doing what bees do, and thought that this in its way was also a sort of miracle.

The wind picked up.

A leaf swirled over the orchard wall from the direction of the lawn. Olive caught it. She wasn't exactly sure what it was, but she tucked it into the buckles of her dungarees with some of the Pink Lady's fallen blossom and left the apple orchard to search for the tree it had come from.

The tulip tree is one of the fastest growing trees in North America, but it can grow for 15 years before it blooms.

There are just two species of tulip tree.

They grow up to 60 metres.

They live for up to 300 years.

The wood of the tulip tree is also known as canoewood: their large trunks make them perfect to hollow out to make dugout canoes.

TULIP TREE
Liriodendron Tulipifera

Tulip Tree

live was puzzled.

At the northern end of the lawn stood the house, looking exactly as she had left it this morning. At the southern end, close to where she stood beneath the giant elm, an open book lay face down on her mother's favourite sun lounger. Olive recognised the cover. It was the book Lady Josephine's friend had brought her yesterday, as a gift.

She must be back in her own time, then. But there were still two trees to go. And where was everybody?

'Here, and not here,' came a voice. 'Different times, existing at once. Human and tree.'

Olive gazed up at the elm. 'Because you live longer?' she asked.

'In polite circles,' said the voice, 'it's good manners to look at the tree you are addressing.'

Olive's hand flew to the leaf in her buckle. She pulled it out and looked at it. Definitely not an elm leaf. What, then? She took a few steps towards a small ornamental maple.

There was a long, rippling sigh.

Olive looked up at the copper beech, tall and magnificently purple.

'Better,' acknowledged the voice. 'I mean, wrong. But closer in size and splendour.'

'Oh, I know who you are!' cried Olive. 'You should have said you were splendid.'

And she ran to the famous tulip tree.

Everyone loved the tulip tree, even Olive's father. For most of the year (though perhaps Olive wouldn't say so out loud) it was just quietly elegant, with a smooth grey trunk and leaves which rustled satisfyingly in the breeze. But when it flowered! Ah, when it flowered its blooms were like a cross between a giant water lily and a huge, showy, cream and gold tulip.

Olive's mother
actually threw parties
for her friends to come and
admire them. She said they
were the sort of flower to celebrate.
The sort of flower to always put a smile
on your face.

The sort of flower, Olive realised with
a pang, which belonged to the sort of tree
her parents would never cut down.

But why was the tulip tree not
talking to her? What should she say?

'If you please, may I have a
story?' she asked, at last.

'Of course,' said the tree.
'Since you ask so nicely.'

There was a little rustling and
creaking from the tulip tree as
Olive chose a spot to sit. When she
had settled down (cross-legged and
careful not to slouch) the sixth story began.

'A LONG TIME AGO, there were two children, a girl called Imogen and a boy called George. They were twins, but very different. Imogen loved studying. George loved nature. Two halves of a whole, their mother used to say, because the twins were devoted to each other. Imogen helped her brother with his schoolwork and showed him the wonders that can be found in books. George dragged his sister outside to explore, showed her birds' nests and badger setts, tiny orchids and towering trees. And so they both grew fit and healthy in body and mind, until the day of the terrible accident.'

Olive gasped.

The tulip tree paused.

'Sorry,' said Olive. 'I didn't mean to interrupt.'

'It was a beautiful day. The sun was shining, the air was clear and blue. As soon as lessons were over – George and Imogen learned at home rather than going to school – they ran outside to play. It was a perfect day for climbing, George said.

On a day like this, from the top of the tallest tree in the park, they would be able to see for miles.

Across the lawn they ran, George in his short trousers, Imogen in a blue dress and petticoats, her long hair tied up by a ribbon...

(... and far be it for me to comment,' the tulip tree interrupted itself, 'but a dress does seem a poor choice for climbing trees.'

'I couldn't agree more,' said Olive.)

George arrived first at the foot of the elm. As he waited for Imogen, he rested his chin on the rough bark and gazed up. Even though his feet were firmly on the ground, just looking at the tree above made him feel as if he was flying. It was one of George's favourite feelings.

Imogen caught up. For a moment, she too rested her chin against the elm and gazed at the high branches.

'It's like a ladder into the sky,' she said.

'Let's climb!'

George jumped
and caught the lowest
branch with his two
hands, swung his legs
and wrapped them
monkey-style around
the branch, then
twisted himself up to
sitting. Imogen joined
him a moment later,
her face flushed, her
hair escaping its
ribbon, her skirts
already in a
tangle.

'All right?'
George asked.

'Never
better!' Imogen
panted.

George reached
for the next branch,
raised his right foot
to a knot in the

trunk, pulled himself up, reached for another branch, folded himself over it, swung his leg neatly across the stump of a broken branch, stood, reached again...
This was his element, what he loved most – this sense that he and the tree were one.

He did not look back.

Behind her twin, Imogen reached for the next branch, raised her right foot to the knot in the trunk, pulled herself up, reached for another branch, folded herself over it, swung her leg...

Oh, her stupid dress!

It did not pass neatly across the stump of broken branch but caught fast on it instead. Imogen pulled and tugged to break free, until at last with a RIP she tore it off...

Slipped...

And...

OUF

OW

BUMP

CRASHED through the branches and landed with a

THUMP
on the lawn
where she lay
still and lifeless
as a CORPSE...
Poor George was convinced that he had killed his sister.'

'Poor George!' cried Olive. 'What about poor Imogen?'

'Oh, Imogen! She'd only broken her leg. Imagine if a tree made a fuss each time we broke a limb! Anyway, that break was the making of her. A doctor came and set her leg. She was left with a limp, but also a burning ambition to become a doctor herself. Not an easy thing for a girl in those days, but she did it. As soon as she was well enough, she went back to her books and studied like mad until at last she graduated from medical school. Her parents threw a party to celebrate. Oh, no, don't feel sorry for Imogen! She isn't even the point of this story. The point of the story, for now, is George.

For months after his twin's accident, poor George would wake every night screaming from nightmares. He blamed himself for her accident, haunted by thoughts he might have lost her. It didn't matter how often she told him it wasn't his fault. After the fall, he turned his back on the natural world. It was too dangerous, too unpredictable. Instead, he forced himself to study. Later, as Imogen followed her heart's desire to become a doctor, George got a job in a bank. A good job, for a person who likes to add up numbers. Certainly a safe job. No chance of hurting yourself in a bank, unless you manage to stab

yourself with an over-sharpened pencil. And so the boy who had spent his childhood roaming forests and meadows looking for butterflies and beetles, scaling trees to the canopy – that boy lived indoors now, and hardly ever went outside.

It was perfectly obvious to everyone that he was dying of boredom.

On the day of Imogen's graduation party, as her guests enjoyed themselves, she went to join her brother under the giant elm, where all his troubles began.

'I was thinking about the accident,' he said (George *always* thought about the accident when he saw his twin). And then, drearily, for at least the thousandth time, 'Will you ever forgive me?'

Instead of replying, Imogen gave him a piece of paper.

It was an advertisement cut from a newspaper, and this is what it said:

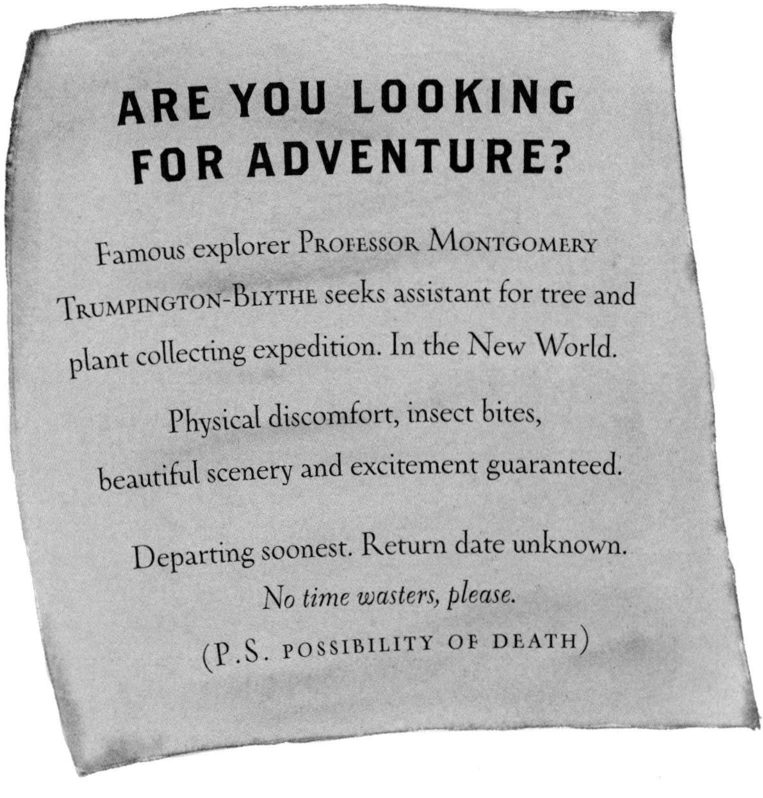

ARE YOU LOOKING FOR ADVENTURE?

Famous explorer PROFESSOR MONTGOMERY TRUMPINGTON-BLYTHE seeks assistant for tree and plant collecting expedition. In the New World.

Physical discomfort, insect bites, beautiful scenery and excitement guaranteed.

Departing soonest. Return date unknown.
No time wasters, please.
(P.S. POSSIBILITY OF DEATH)

'If you don't apply,'
said Imogen, 'then I will
never forgive you.'

A month later, George set
sail for the New World. Imogen
went to wave him off at the docks.

'Bring me something pretty!' she said as
she hugged him, and he promised.

Now, by this stage of their evolution, most
humans were travelling by steam ship. Professor
Trumpington-Blythe (let's call him Monty) preferred
to sail. People laughed at him, but I applaud his
choice.

Unlike steam, wind does not
pollute.

The ocean crossing
took six weeks, and
it was the most
exciting time
George had
ever had. Some
people find sea
travel dull, but
not George!

George was thrilled by it! From the moment he set foot on the Spirit of Discovery, he felt alive again. He spent hours on deck. He saw dolphins, porpoises, whales and flying fish. He watched the colour of the water change from blue to gold as the sun set, to milky white at dawn. And when he wasn't doing this, he was working, poring over the enormous books Monty had brought with him on the expedition.

This was the age of the Great Plant Hunters. Oh, don't be alarmed! The hunters weren't trying to kill us! They were collecting us – gathering seeds and cuttings from around the world to bring back to their own countries. Sometimes because the plants were useful for medicine or science. Sometimes simply because they were beautiful and people would pay well to have them in their parks and gardens. The great thing was to discover a type of plant before anyone else did, and to give it your name.

This was what
Monty wanted,
and the reason
George was
studying those books was
to learn what had already been
discovered.

It's absurd, of course. As if somehow
plants don't exist until humans have
discovered them! Why, there are over two
hundred species of magnolia alone – I
myself am one of the more impressive
examples. George, however, did not see
the absurdity of hunting for a flower in
order to name it. Quite the contrary! The
idea gripped him like a fever – here at last was
something he could do for Imogen! He would not
simply bring her back something pretty, as she had
asked. He would bring back something unique –
something he would discover – and he would name it
just for her.

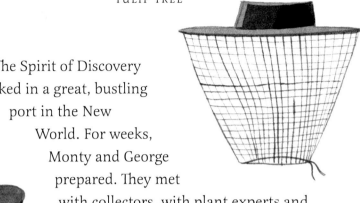

The Spirit of Discovery
docked in a great, bustling
port in the New
World. For weeks,
Monty and George
prepared. They met
with collectors, with plant experts and
explorers. They bought boots and insect
repellent, a stout tent, hundreds of
envelopes in which to store the seeds they
gathered, and tin boxes in which to keep
the envelopes dry. They bought water bottles
and saucepans, sleeping bags and mosquito nets,
until at last, almost a month after they had
landed, they were off!

For over a year they travelled, by
train, by boat, by horse, by canoe. Being
an explorer was as tough as Monty had
described in his advertisement – and George
loved it! His life was as dangerous and exciting
now as before it had been safe and dull.

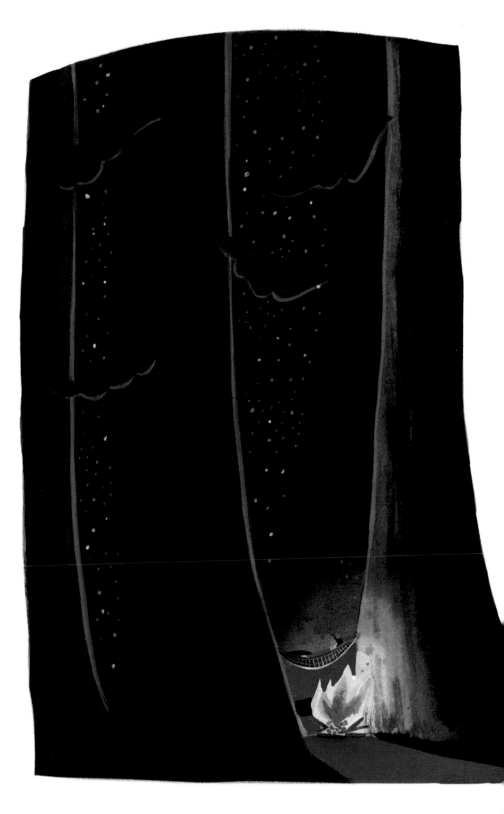

George pitched tents and slung hammocks, he shot pigeons and squirrels to roast over campfires, he dressed blisters the size of boiled eggs and learned how to smoke out mosquitoes. He caught dysentery after failing to boil drinking water, his leg swelled to twice its size because of a mysterious insect bite, he mistook a poisonous blue berry for bilberries and vomited for a week. But almost every night, when the fire went out and darkness fell, he lay in his hammock or on the cold hard earth and marvelled at the stars.

And best of all there were the trees. Giant sequoias which soared higher than the tallest buildings with trunks as wide as a small room, sweet maples he could tap for delicious syrup, forests which blazed like fire in the autumn, orange groves which stretched as far as the eye could see... George and Monty recorded everything they learned, sketched, photographed, interviewed locals to learn their names and uses, collected bark samples, pressed flowers, gathered seeds and labelled envelopes. Their notes and their collection grew, and it was wonderful, but...

Humans!

All the time,
something rankled.
Something prickled and niggled.

They had not discovered a plant they wanted for their own. To be sure, they found plants they didn't know. Insignificant little flowers, a mushroom or two. But Monty wanted something spectacular, and George wanted something worthy of his sister, and nothing was ever quite good enough.

In the end, they ran out of money. And so Monty and George sold the tent and the sleeping bags, the mosquito nets and the saucepans. Then, with their notes and seeds and cuttings and pressed flowers gathered in a large chest, they returned to the great port where they had first docked and boarded the Spirit of Discovery. George's heart was heavy. He knew he should be feeling proud and grateful for this year of adventures, but all he could think was that he had failed.

They had one afternoon left in the New World. George spent it at the Botanical Gardens, where he sat upon a bench and thought gloomy thoughts of failure. A cone had fallen from the tree above him. Out of habit, George prised out some of its seeds and put them into an envelope which he slipped into his coat pocket.

Ah, the Spirit of Discovery! How different things might have been if Monty hadn't preferred sail to steam! Shortly after her departure, for two precious days, the Discovery was becalmed off the coast of the New World. On the third day, the wind picked up again, but already it was too late. A giant iceberg had detached itself from the mainland, and was drifting towards them...

'No!' gasped Olive.

'Yes!' said the tulip tree.

Everything was lost. The Spirit of Discovery, most of her passengers and crew. And the chest containing an entire year's work, carried away by the waves.

Monty and George survived though. And in George's coat pocket...

'The seeds,' breathed Olive.

'The seeds,' said the tulip tree.

And now for the beautiful part.

George returned home overcome with embarrassment. Nothing to show for his year away but a few seeds!

'They probably won't even sprout,' he warned Imogen. 'They got so wet. They're probably dead.'

But every day at the hospital where she worked, Imogen saw how stubbornly sick patients clung to life.

'You never know,' she said. 'Let's plant them and see.'

Together, the twins wrapped the seeds in damp cotton wool and put them on a shelf in a heated greenhouse.

Some of the seeds were dead, but a few germinated. The twins planted these in compost plugs. A few more died, but once the survivors had sprouted, George and Imogen transferred the seedlings to small pots, and then to bigger ones. Three years after George's return, they selected the healthiest sapling – and planted it where it stands now, where everyone who comes to the house can admire its splendour...

'Wait a minute!' Olive interrupted. 'That tree was you?'

Like a preening bird, the tulip tree rustled.

'It was. And there in that spot I carried on growing, more splendid by the day. The year after George died, I flowered and Imogen was absolutely enchanted...'

'George died?' cried Olive. 'Before he saw you flower? That is a terrible story.'

'It's a miraculous story!' The tulip tree sounded astonished. 'I survived! And like I said, Imogen was enchanted. She said I was the prettiest tree she had ever seen, and she buried George's ashes in my roots. You're actually sitting on him now.'

Olive squeaked and shuffled aside.

'You might have flowered sooner,' she said. 'After everything George did for you!'

'I didn't ask George to collect me,' the tulip tree retorted. 'He chose to. No one knows what would have happened if he hadn't come along. I might have decomposed, or I might have sprouted. Either way I would have done it without him. Trees don't exist to serve humans, you know, whatever humans think. We're not here for you to write poems about us, or to make you rich, or to absorb the carbon you produce. We're not responsible for you. But you... when you choose to meddle with us, then you become responsible for us. It's your duty to care for us, not the other way around.'

Olive thought for a while in silence, feeling rather small.

'Do you know how many sorts of oak tree there are?' she asked at last.

'About six hundred, I believe,' said the tulip tree. 'They're very common.'

'It doesn't mean they're not precious though, does it? Just because they're common?'

'No,' agreed the tulip tree. 'Every tree is precious. Every tree is different, just as every human is.'

'That's what I think too,' said Olive. 'Thank you, tulip tree.'

But already the clock in the tower was striking for the sixth time.

Olive looked, but there was no leaf, no seed, to show her where to go next.

Only a new voice, carried on the breeze.

You are most likely to see box in gardens as hedges, often cut into interesting shapes.

There are about 70 species of box.

They can grow up to 9 metres.

They live for several hundred years.

Trees have rings in their trunks, which show how old they are – a ring for every year. Box grows very slowly, so its rings are very close together making it especially tough.

Box
Buxus Sempervirens

Box

'Over here! Over here!'

If you had asked Olive what made a voice sound like a tree, she couldn't have told you exactly. A sort of breathiness, maybe, plus of course that strange in-her-head-but-not quality. This new voice was definitely not a tree. It was human, a boy, and it sounded terrified.

Where was it coming from?

'Over here!'

The river! Olive broke into a run.

'I'm coming!' she shouted as she ran.

But there was nobody there when she reached the bridge, and now the voice was calling from the other side of the river, always the same words, more and

more urgent. Olive ran again, and didn't stop until she reached a small wood, where she slowed to listen.

'Where are you?' she shouted. 'Are you all right?'

'Over here!'

A path wound through the wood. Olive knew it well. It was the one she took to visit her oak tree, but she'd never stopped here before. Now as she walked she peered into the undergrowth. Hazel, holly, willow, birch – where was the boy?

Should she leave the path and search among the trees? Deep inside Olive's mind a warning bell rang, a long-held memory of stories in which bad things happened to people who strayed from forest paths. But what could happen to her here? There were no wolves, no witches...

There's magic, rang the warning bell...

'Over here!' the boy called.

Close – there, beyond that clearing, in a dark, dark thicket...

Olive left the path and began to run.

⁕⁕⁕

As soon as she entered the thicket, Olive knew she had made a mistake. Birds stopped singing, the air grew cold, the sky all but disappeared. The trees were about twice her height, planted close together, with tough leathery leaves the size of an adult thumbnail. Their trunks twisted and coiled above her like snakes, reaching for the sky blocked out by the canopy of other, taller trees. There was a path of sorts among them, but it made no sense. It twisted left, then right, then stopped. Olive tried to turn back – left, right... The path stopped again.

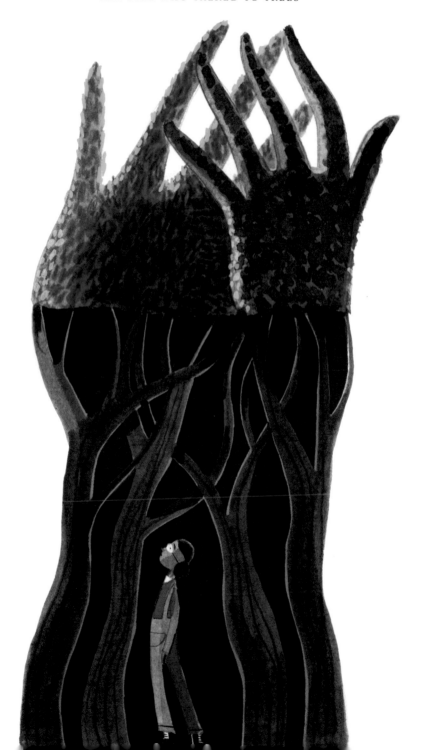

Right, left – stop. Left, left, right – right, left – left again, and suddenly the path opened up and she was in a clearing, at the centre of which stood a broken sundial.

What was this place? Olive was almost certain she would never find her way back out. She took a deep breath, trying not to panic. There was a perfume, sweet and heady like lilies, but not lilies, further muddling her brain. It conjured images of well-ordered flower beds and tidy hedges and... a peacock? Yes, a peacock, running over a neatly trimmed hedge, with another peacock running towards it and between them three giant dancing mice.

Olive pressed her face in her hands.

Where was she? And where was the calling boy?

Close behind her, she heard a laugh. She whipped round.

'Who's there?'

Another laugh, behind her again.

'Who are you? Where's the boy?'

'Over here! Over here! Over here!'

The call echoed around her. Olive turned again and again. There was no one there. No one but the trees, the twisting, snaking trees.

'You tricked me!'

She felt afraid, but clenched her fists, trying to look angry. The little trees rattled with laughter.

'It's not funny!' said Olive.

'Yes, it is,' hissed a voice behind her. Olive spun, then shrank back as leaves brushed against her face. 'Humans are always making us into things we're not. We're only doing what we've been trained to do.'

'You're speaking in riddles.'

'We are box trees. Trees. Once we grew wild all over this continent, until humans decided they had

a better use for us. You see us as hedges, borders for flowers and vegetables. Cut into balls and keys and birds...'

A branch cracked, as if the tree were spitting.

The peacocks and the dancing mice! Now Olive remembered – she had seen them on a visit with her mother to family friends. Lady Josephine had thought them charming, especially the mice. 'It's called topiary,' Lady Josephine had said. 'The art of clipping trees and shrubs into shapes. Isn't it clever?'

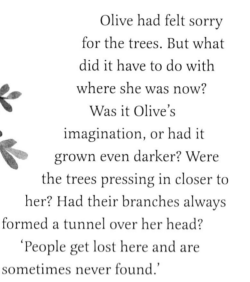

Olive had felt sorry
for the trees. But what
did it have to do with
where she was now?
Was it Olive's
imagination, or had it
grown even darker? Were
the trees pressing in closer to
her? Had their branches always
formed a tunnel over her head?
'People get lost here and are
sometimes never found.'
'Lost... lost... lost...'
The cry rippled mournfully around the
clearing. Olive swallowed.
'Is this a maze?'
'It is, and you are at the centre of it.'
Olive tried to keep her voice steady.
'I'd like to go now, please.'
'Sit down,' ordered the tree.
'Let me tell you a story.'

THERE WAS ONCE A MAN who thought he could control the world.

He was in every way a powerful man. Physically, he was tall, with strong legs and broad shoulders. Although he was well into middle age at the time of this story, he appeared much younger. Every morning when he got up, in winter as in spring, he ran around his estate, and finished his run with a dive in his river. When his hair grew grey, he dyed it. When it fell out, he ordered a wig made from the hair of men half his age. When he developed wrinkles, he had them filled in with special injections.

In this way, he controlled time.

This man – his name was Henry – owned a great deal of land. And on this land were many farms and cottages. Everyone who lived in them had to swear obedience to him and give him three quarters of the food they grew, even if it meant they starved. If they didn't, he threw them out of their homes.

In this way, he controlled people.

The parts of Henry's land which weren't farmed
for food were given over to his pleasure. When he
first came there, he ripped out the gardens which had
been planted before him. The previous owners had
allowed these gardens to grow almost wild, with roses
tumbling through trees and drifts of snowdrops and
primroses and cyclamen across the lawn. They had
left the woods largely untouched, doing only what
was necessary to keep the trees healthy, so that they
looked as they had for centuries, alive with birdsong
and animals.

Henry built beds for new plants in straight, strict rows. He cut down the woods. And in a clearing which had once been wild he planted us, in a circular pattern of his own devising, with paths which led, after many twists and turns, to a sundial. As we grew he clipped us and cut us to look like a wall, as smooth and lifeless as brick.

And so Henry controlled nature.

It did not occur to him that one day nature might fight back.

Now, Henry had a son, a boy called Bruno. And
naturally, Henry controlled him. Bruno's mother,
Mathilde, had been a singer, but she had died when
he was a baby. The boy inherited her sweet smile, her
large, brown eyes, her dreamy nature and her voice.
But we'll come back to that later. For now, picture
him as a little child for whom almost everything
was forbidden. Henry decided what Bruno ate for
breakfast, where he went on his walks, what books
he read, what sports he did. One day, Bruno would
inherit the house and lands. When he did, Henry
wanted him to be identical to him in every way,
so that even when he was dead Henry would be in
control.

Bruno was absolutely not allowed to sing.

For years, every minute of Bruno's time was controlled by Henry. It never occurred to him to rebel.

Nobody rebelled against Henry.

But then, shortly after Bruno's eleventh birthday, Henry went away for a week on business. And on a rainy day, when Bruno's tutor had gone to bed to nurse a bad cold and Bruno could not go out with him for a walk, he decided instead to explore...

Over the house he went, tiptoeing into rooms where he wasn't allowed to go – the library with the books he was banned from reading, the study where his father must not be disturbed, the kitchen pantry where there was food he was not supposed to eat – until at last he came to his mother's old music room, where among the dusty instruments he discovered a record player and a collection of his mother's records.

Oh, what an afternoon he had!

Bruno played every single one of his mother's records, again and again, in a sort of trance. He had never heard anything so beautiful in his life. His mother sang sad songs about love and loss, and a funny song about people trying to say goodbye at a railway station, and a song about the sun and the moon rising over a hillside which was so haunting it made his heart ache.

There and then he decided that he too would be a singer like her.

Every day for a week, he returned to the music room to play his mother's songs. He wrote down the words. He memorised the melodies. The servants heard but did nothing to stop him – it was so long since there had been music in the house! The tutor recovered from his cold, but he did nothing either, for he too was a lover of music. Bruno sang everywhere. In the bath, on his walks, on his way to meals. He hummed as he worked at his lessons. He whistled as he fenced and boxed.

The days passed.

᪥᪥᪥

Henry returned
unexpectedly early, in a mood
because his business trip had ended
badly. The first thing he heard when he came
home was Bruno singing his mother's songs.

Henry flew into a rage. He fired the tutor.
He raged at the servants. He smashed the
instruments, he broke the records, he kicked the
record player to pieces.

And Bruno?

Bruno wept, but he was brave. 'I don't care
what you say,' he shouted. 'You will
never stop me singing!'

And then he ran.

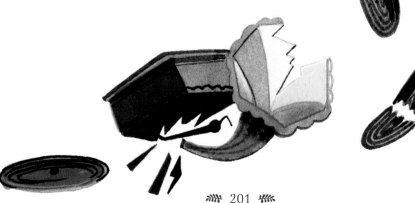

Out into the formal garden he went, over the river, through the woods and to us.

Where better to hide than in the heart of a maze?

Bruno knew us well – after all, he had grown up with us. Right, left, left, right, through a special shortcut he had made under a hedge, right, left, left again until he reached the sundial at the centre, where he threw himself down and wept again.

We watched in silence.

When Bruno had finished weeping, he curled into a ball. Hunched against the sundial, he looked up at the sky.

'I'll show him!' he vowed. 'I will be a singer.'

The day moved on, lingered a while and died.

Bruno shivered. What should he do now, with an angry father at home and a cold dark night ahead?

What could he do, but sing?

Bruno sang the song he loved the best from all his mother's records, about the sun and the moon rising and falling. His voice was weak at first, after so much crying. He poured his sadness into it but it did not touch us. Why should it? What was the point of singing about the sun and the moon? Is it not enough that they exist? Is it not enough, to celebrate them,

to gaze upon the silvery woods at night? To wait until dawn once again paints them with its colours?

That is what we thought of Bruno's singing, at first. But as night deepened, his voice began to warm. He stood and turned his face to the stars.

'I will be a singer,' he repeated, and his voice swelled like a river after rain.

Bruno's singing was the hush of winter snow and the trill of the summer nightingale, it was the growth of leaves in spring and the whisper of their fall in autumn. It was all these things and more. An enchantment, a magic spell.

Which explains, perhaps, what happened next.

Up at the house,
Henry was still furious, but
by dusk when Bruno did not return,
he began to worry. Servants searched for
Bruno far and wide, from the cellars to the
attic, in the gardens and farmland and orchard
and meadows. Henry joined in the search, shouting
orders.

Night fell, and the servants turned for home. There
would be no finding Bruno in the dark.

The singing began as they approached the bridge.

For as long as they lived, the servants never forgot
that singing.

Henry, pacing up and down the terrace at the top
of the lawn, also heard his son.

Bruno's song soared, carried by our sighs,
the running river, the call of night birds. But it
did not enchant Henry as it had enchanted us.
Away he marched from the house, down to
the river and over the bridge. In among us he
strode, swiping the riding crop he always carried,
slicing through leaves, breaking off branches.
Hurting us. Remember that when you hear
what happened next.

Hurting us.

Bruno had frozen at the sound of his father's
approach. He needed to run but appeared to have
grown roots.

'Go... go... go...' we urged, but he did not hear us.
'We will stop him stop him stop him...'

CRACK!

Another swipe of the whip.
More leaves tumbled to the ground
and
Bruno
ran...

The boy knew the maze like the back of his hand, but his father knew our secrets too. There was only one way in and out. Sooner or later, father and son would meet.

CRACK, THWACK, went the riding whip, and we trembled for Bruno.

So we... helped.

Here we entwined our branches to close off a path to Henry. There we bowed to let Bruno through. Nimbly, he ran and jumped and ducked and dived, while Henry crashed and blundered and swore, as our poor clipped limbs awakened.

Once started, revenge is hard to stop.

Bruno staggered out of the maze and ran.

We kept Henry... a little longer.

'Just until Bruno gets away,' we murmured. Let him pack his bags and leave, go far away with the music-loving tutor, find his mother's family perhaps, who can help him to sing...

Or until he returns, maybe, to sing to us again.

Henry lost his whip. His face and hands bled from fighting us.

'Bruno!' he shouted. 'I'm sorry! Bruno, where are you?'

'Over here...' we replied, in Bruno's voice.

'Over here... over here...'

The box tree fell silent. Olive gave herself a shake, like someone just waking up, and saw that the little sunlight there had been in the twisted trees was gone.

And had the trees grown once more? Had their branches always interlaced so tightly around her, almost like - no, exactly like - a cage?

'Did Bruno...' Olive swallowed. Her throat for some reason was very dry. 'Did he return?'

'He did not.'

'And Henry... where is he?'

'Over here!' a man's voice cried out.

'Over here...

over here...'

'We told you, did we not, that nature would fight back?'

'Please let me go,' Olive whispered.

'Why should we?'

'I'll sing to you!' Olive croaked. 'Like Bruno did, a magic song full of spring and summer and

autumn and winter and the moon and the sun and nightingales—'

But even as she said this, Olive knew that a song wouldn't do. Unlike Bruno, she was not a singer.

What, then?

'Because I made a promise,' she said. 'That when the time came, I would speak up. And because I have so many stories to tell.'

'Ah, stories...'

The trees sighed.

'A story is like a song...'

The branches of the box trees parted.

In the distance, the clock in the tower sounded for the last time.

The Girl Who Talked to Trees

O live came out of the woods
bedraggled and dirty, with hair full
of twigs and hands covered in cuts,
but walking taller than when she had
run away from the breakfast table that morning.

She stopped when she reached the bridge to
watch the river and thought of the alder tree,
dreaming of the ocean. Turned and looked past the
box trees' woods towards the farmland which had
once been a forest. Closed her eyes and thought
of the dear linden, the majestic oak, all the vast
beautiful trees. Wondered, were she to walk over
the land where once they'd stood, she would feel
their ghosts.

But she
had a promise
to keep.
She left the
bridge and
entered the
parkland.
Stopped again
briefly at the end
of the path which
led to the plane tree
and thought of the
storyteller who once,
in a distant city, had
drawn on the wisdom
of trees to stop a
war. Lingered
by the orchard
wall in the hope of
catching some apple
tree gossip,

walked on past the elm
out of which Imogen had
fallen, greeted the tulip
tree with a respectful
nod, and at last reached
the top of the lawn
where she looked again
back at the valley.

In the meadow on the
other side of the river,
the oak tree she loved waited.

'Olive!' Her mother's voice
called from the terrace
where the family were
gathering for tea.
'Where have you
been all day?'

Olive knew what
she had to do.

It took her a while to be able to do it.

First, there were the cries of horror at her appearance.

'You look like you've been dragged through a hedge!' cried Lady Josephine. ('I have,' said Olive.) And, 'Have you been swimming in your clothes?' asked Rosa. ('Sort of,' said Olive.) And, 'You're covered in cuts!' exclaimed Nana. ('I know,' said Olive. 'It doesn't matter.')

Then, when that was over, there was a difficult moment when Sir Sydney (predictably) denied he had ever made any promise to Olive.

'You must have imagined it,' said Sir Sydney. 'That doesn't sound like me at all.'

A butler came out of the house carrying a tray with
cups and saucers, followed by an under-butler with a
teapot and a maid with a plate of pastries stuffed with
nuts and honey.

Olive's eyes widened, but she was not to be
distracted.

She took a pastry, because she was starving, and
she drank some tea. And when she had finished, she
put down her plate and cup and said, 'Let me tell you
a story.'

The tea was drunk, the cakes were eaten, the tea things cleared away. The afternoon light mellowed, the shadows of the great elm and the tulip tree stretched across the lawn. The air grew colder. The butler brought snacks and drinks. The under-butler brought blankets. The maid brought candles. Eventually, they ran out of things to bring but stayed to listen anyway, because the Girl Who Talked to Trees was telling the most incredible, most wild, most wonderful stories.

On and on Olive talked, as day turned to night and the first evening stars prickled the sky. About the ancient oak and the hunters and the storm on the forest floor. About the giant linden and trees that went on for ever. About underwater forests and mermaids, and mountains covered in apple blossom, and George's years of adventuring to bring home the tulip tree, and the peace big trees bring to busy cities, and Bruno singing in the maze. And through it she told them another story, of a forest disappearing and a changing landscape. She told them about all the life that is supported by the forest, and that trees don't belong to anyone, not really, and that every tree is different. She spoke of valuing the treasure you

have rather than chasing after new riches, and of the
responsibility we have towards the things we change.

She spoke of nature fighting back.

Last of all, she talked about her oak, and how
it had grown from an acorn into one of the last
survivors of an ancient world, and how she would not
let her father destroy it.

Night had fallen by the time she finished.

'Did all this really happen?' whispered Rosa.

'Yes,' said Olive.

'Nonsense!' said Sir Sydney, a bit shakily.

'Talking trees!'

Everyone shot him a look, even the
servants.

'Even if it were true,'
grumbled Sir Sydney,

'what do you want
me to do?

Is Olive expected to
impress my guests with stories
every time they visit?'

'If you want me to, I will,' said Olive.
'But I'll tell you something else you can do.
Something really impressive.'

'Go on,' said her father.

'Plant a new forest,' said Olive.

When at last everyone had left the terrace and
gone indoors, Olive slipped away in the moonlight to
the meadow and her solitary oak. She climbed up on
to her favourite branch and lay on her back to look at
the stars through the leaves.

'We did it,' she whispered. 'All of us together, we
saved you.'

The oak tree didn't speak, not in the way it had
that morning, when she met it as a tiny seedling.
But somewhere in the rustling branches she heard
its answer.

'You were right,' the oak sighed through the
fluttering wind. 'I did become magnificent.'

What Happened Next

FOR YEARS AFTERWARDS, when guests came to the grand old house, Sir Sydney marched them down the lawn and across the bridge to the meadow where saplings grew, hazel and birch and linden and oak, every year a little taller. He would point across to the farm fields where little by little more trees were being planted, and explain how once all of this land had been covered in trees and how it would be again. And do you know what?

His guests were impressed.

If Olive was home, Sir Sydney – proud father and grower of trees – would ask her to tell her stories, and she always did so willingly. But as Olive grew up, she was home less and less. When she finished school, she studied with experts all over the world. She wrote many books, and planted many trees, and thanks to her, whole hillsides were covered with forests – not as big as the one she saw from the top of the linden tree, but it was a start.

She became very famous indeed out in the world, but at home she was always known as the Girl Who Talked to Trees.

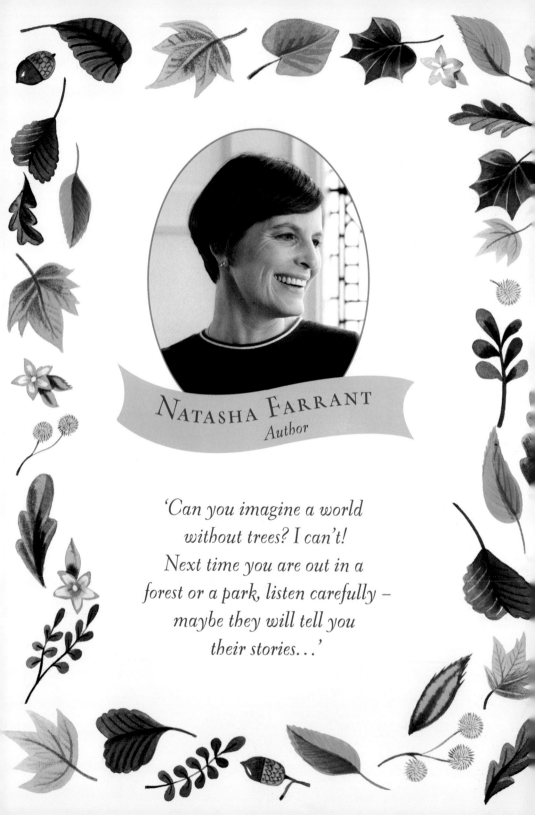

NATASHA FARRANT
Author

'Can you imagine a world
without trees? I can't!
Next time you are out in a
forest or a park, listen carefully –
maybe they will tell you
their stories...'

LYDIA CORRY
Illustrator

'The best place in the
world to read a book is
under the shade of a tree.
How magic they are –
can you feel it?'

'*Mirror, mirror on the wall...*
what makes a princess excellent?'

Eight Princesses and a Magic Mirror
IS OUT NOW

THE ENCHANTRESS AND THE MAGIC MIRROR

Once upon a time, in a faraway place, a king and a queen asked a powerful enchantress to be godmother to their baby daughter. The enchantress replied that she would be delighted, and promised to help her goddaughter become an excellent princess.

But later, as she was getting ready for bed, the enchantress wondered what she had let herself in for.

'An excellent princess,' she mused. 'What does that actually mean?'

'It means,' scolded a maid, as she tugged a brush through the enchantress's tangled hair, 'that she must be pretty.'

'And tidy,' grumbled another maid, picking up the

THE PRINCESS OF ABSOLUTE LOVELINESS

High on the tallest of the Central Mountains nestles the ancient city of Bamfou. Forest stretches into the clouds above it, and far below, sea the colour of sapphires glitters and breaks on dark branches. But it is the river which flows around the city in lazy loops that allows it to thrive. The people of Bamfou have planted gardens on its banks, where they grow rice and yams and okra, coffee and berries and melon. Legend says the river is guarded by a shaman who lives in the forest, a wise woman over a thousand years old. For the most part, she does an excellent job of keeping the water flowing pure and sweet, never too slow nor too fast. Every few years, when the rains come, and the river bursts its

horrible. Princess! Not like a real friend at all!'

'My board smashed,' Karim grumbled. 'And I can't afford another one.'

Katy's phone pinged. 'Agnieszka's coming home! Tomorrow! Oh, there's another message, I missed it, at seven-thirty – she says she's homesick...' Katy frowned. 'Seven-thirty. That's when I left Melody's...'

'It's the time I fell off my board,' said Karim.

Princess's heart missed a beat.

Seven-thirty – the time on the station clock when the old woman disappeared.

'How strange,' Katy said. 'But, oh, how good that we'll be together again! Everything back to normal.'

She hugged Princess. 'I'm sorry,' she said. 'I was horrible. I love you.'

'I'm sorry too,' said Karim. 'I mean, I don't think I was horrible. But I'm sorry I haven't been around.'

Together, they went into the garden, and lay on the grass in the darkening twilight.

Everything back to normal, thought Princess. Except it wasn't, was it? Because the notice was still there, nailed to the gate.

And she had thought a garden could last for ever!

The liquid-gold notes of a bird spilled into the air, and that was strange too because she had never heard it before.

'It's like music,' sighed Karim, and when had Karim ever noticed a bird?

'Like magic,' breathed Katy. 'Like magic music.'

Princess's idea shot through her like a lightning bolt.

She knew exactly what to do to save the garden.

'You want to find an old homeless woman and ask her to play in a concert?' Katy's eyes couldn't have been any wider.

Zephyr is an imprint of Head of Zeus.
At Zephyr we are proud to publish
books you can read and re-read time
and time again because they tell
a brilliant story and because they
entertain you.

🐦 @_ZephyrBooks

📷 _zephyrbooks

📘 HeadofZeusBooks

readzephyr.com
www.headofzeus.com

ZEPHYR